"You're a woman with needs of her own."

"I can't afford those needs," she cried. "Jake, go home, back to your motel. Back to New York or Singapore or wherever it is you hang out."

"I'm in no state to walk out the door."

She flushed scarlet, turned to the sink and plunged her hands in. "My life was nicely in order until you turned up. But now I don't even know which way's up."

Entranced, Jake said, "Is that what you want on your tombstone? 'I had an orderly life'?" As she plunked a couple of plates into the rack, he added, "Fantasizing about breaking those over my head?"

"It's the other fantasies I can't deal with."

Sandra Field

SURRENDER TO MARRIAGE

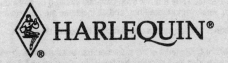

TORONTO • NEW YORK • LONDON
AMSTERDAM • PARIS • SYDNEY • HAMBURG
STOCKHOLM • ATHENS • TOKYO • MILAN • MADRID
PRAGUE • WARSAW • BUDAPEST • AUCKLAND

ISBN 0-373-12443-0

SURRENDER TO MARRIAGE

First North American Publication 2005.

www.eHarlequin.com

Printed in U.S.A.

CHAPTER ONE

Jake Reilly pulled over to the side of the road and got out of his vehicle. His leather loafers crunching on the dirt shoulder, he walked to the crest of the hill, where the sea wind tugged at his thick dark hair. The ocean stretched as far as he could see, a white lace of surf edging the cliffs and the island at the mouth of the cove.

The island where, long ago, he'd made love with Shaine.

His mouth tightened. Almost against his will, his gaze dropped from the dark turquoise water to the little Newfoundland village huddled along the shoreline, surrounded by a dark ruff of spruce and fir. He'd been away for thirteen years, yet he could have named the owner of each of the neatly painted houses, with their picket fences and chimneys breathing blue wood smoke. But it was the house nearest the cliff path that drew his eyes like a magnet. The house where Shaine had lived. Shaine, her parents and her three brothers, Devlin, Padric and Connor. Redheads all of them, although none like her, whose hair had been like the flames of driftwood burning on the beach, vivid and glinting with gold...

Jake jammed his hands in his pockets, swearing under his breath as he forced himself to look away from the yellow-painted house that belonged to the O'Sullivans. The bungalow where he'd grown up, as an only child, was closer to the road; his mother had sold it after she'd moved to Australia and remarried. She'd phoned him, Jake remembered, to make sure he didn't want to keep the place for himself. "Are you kidding?" he'd said. "I doubt I'll ever go there again...there's nothing in the village for me, why would I go back?"

Why, indeed. So what was he doing here now? Why, on a sunny day early in September, was he standing like a lump of granite by the side of the road that led to Cranberry Cove, when he could have been anywhere else in the world? Windsurfing off the beach of his luxurious mansion in the Hamptons on Long Island. Going to the theater in New York City, then staying at his equally luxurious condo that overlooked Central Park. Wandering the streets of Paris, where he had a flat within walking distance of the Louvre. Or, in a more practical vein, doing business in any of a hundred locations that ranged from Buenos Aires to Oslo.

Shaine, he was certain, would have left the cove years ago. Shaken its dust from her feet much as he had. So he hadn't come back to see her.

He'd probably bump into her brothers, though. If he wanted to, he could ask where she was.

What would he do that for? He didn't want to see Shaine again any more than she'd want to see him. After all, she was the one who'd refused to leave Cranberry Cove with him thirteen years back; who, despite his passionate out-pouring of love, had stayed behind in the village where she'd been born, so that he'd had to leave on his own.

Would he ever forget the raw agony of that rejection?

Maybe, Jake thought slowly, that was one reason why he'd come back here today. To revisit the place where the only woman he'd ever loved had turned her back on him and walked away. As clearly as if it were yesterday, he could see the flutter of her blue dress in the breeze, the tumble of her vivid hair down her back...

Furious with himself, Jake strode back to his rented car and got in behind the wheel. He'd drive around the village, chat with a couple of people and leave this afternoon. He could be back at the airport in time to fly home tonight, this whole ridiculous expedition behind him. His past safely in the past. Where it belonged.

The descent to the village, down Breakheart Hill, took longer than he wanted. For a moment, at the very edge of the houses, Jake stopped again, parking by the curb. He could turn around and hightail it to the airport without anyone even knowing he'd been here. Wouldn't that be the smartest thing to do?

Coward, a little voice sneered in his head. Scared of a few memories? Afraid you'll meet one of Shaine's brothers and find out she's happily married with three or four kids? What kind of a man are you?

To his huge dismay, Jake realized he was afraid. His heart was beating fast in his chest, his fingers knotted around the wheel. The exact same symptoms he'd had each time he'd gone to the O'Sullivans' house to pick up Shaine for a walk along the cliffs, or for a shopping trip in his mother's car into Corner Brook. Had there ever been a woman as beautiful as Shaine O'Sullivan at eighteen? Poised on the threshold of womanhood, innocent and unawakened, yet with an unconscious sensuality that had made his throat ache with longing and his body surge with the need to possess her.

He had possessed her. Once, to be exact.

Jake yanked the keys out of the ignition and got out of the car. It was an unpretentious car, one of the smaller models available at the airport rental agency, and nothing like his beloved silver Ferrari that he kept in his garage in the Hamptons. Just as the clothes he was wearing were also unpretentious. Jeans, an open-necked shirt, and a leather bomber jacket he'd owned for at least five years.

He hadn't wanted to stand out, or to scream his success to anyone he might meet. There was an enormous gap between his lifestyle and that of the villagers whose homely little houses were perched along the cliffs; there was no point in thrusting that gap in their faces. But what Jake was forgetting was the hard-earned aura of confidence, success and worldliness that clung to him like a second skin.

Coupled with this was the subtle sexuality of his tautly molded cheekbones, determined jawline, and smoldering blue eyes, deep-set under hair that had the patina of burnished leather. He could do nothing about any of these externals; so he tended to ignore them as if they didn't exist.

He took a deep breath, his lungs filling with the clean, sharp tang of the sea. Closer, wood smoke from someone's stove mingled with the warm yeasty odour of freshly baked bread. The years kaleidoscoped. He was seventeen again, desperate to escape the confines of the village for the wider world of university. When he was seventeen, Shaine had been thirteen, a girl he'd casually befriended because she, like himself, was different, a misfit in the village, a loner.

He'd gotten away. But then he'd come back five years later, and that was when he'd fallen in love.

Jake started off down the street. Three doors down, an old man was sitting on his front porch in a squeaky rocking chair, the fumes from a foul-smelling pipe overriding the salt-laden breeze. Jake cleared his throat. "Hi there, Abe. Remember me? Jake Reilly. I used to live six houses north of here."

Abe spat accurately into the dahlias that were staked to the porch. "You scored that winning shot against the St. John's team. Won us the provincial hockey trophy." He cackled uncouthly. "There was one helluva party at the legion that night, I'll tell you."

Jake grinned. "First time in my life I got royally drunk. Black Horse beer. I paid for it the next morning—the worst hangover I've ever had. But it was worth it."

"That was some goal," Abe said contentedly. "The stands went wild...so what brings you back to these parts, boy?"

"Just wanted to see the old place again," Jake said vaguely. "Fill me in on all the gossip, Abe."

Abe tamped more tobacco in his pipe, and for the better

part of half an hour talked nonstop, going from house to house in a colorful recital of who had married, been born, or died, with a good many libellous details along the way. The last house on the cliffs was the O'Sullivans'. Jake found he was waiting, his heart once again thudding in his chest.

"The three boys, now they all done fine. Devlin's lobster fishing, Padric's a carpenter and Connor's just out of school, thinking to do one of them fancy computer courses in town. You knew their mum and dad died? Not long after you left, I reckon that would be."

"Shaine's parents died?" Jake croaked.

"That's right. Car skidded on black ice on Breakheart Hill." Abe shook his head. "Broke the gal's heart. She'd gone away to university. But she came home, raised the boys."

Abe shot him a keen glance from beneath his bushy white eyebrows. "You didn't know 'bout any of that?"

"No."

"Well, now. There's always a surprise or two when a fella stays away too long."

Jake glanced up sharply. But Abe was busy with his pipe again, scouring the bowl with his pocket knife. "You figure I should have come home sooner?" Jake said, inwardly disconcerted with how easily the word home slipped from his tongue.

"I never said that," Abe remarked. "You going to see Shaine?"

Jake's jaw dropped. "See her? Where?"

"She still lives in her parents' house. Owns a craft shop at the other end of the street. Doing fine, so I hear. Not much into that kinda stuff myself."

His head reeling, Jake said, "I figured she'd be long gone."

"There's things keep a woman home," Abe said, with another of those unexpectedly shrewd glances. "Now you always had the bug to leave. To go find something you couldn't find here."

"That's right enough."

"So did you find it?"

"You sure ask tough questions," Jake said, not entirely in jest. "I guess I did. Of course I did."

"Make a buck or two?"

Many million, thought Jake. "I've done okay."

"Go buy yourself something from her craft shop then," Abe said. "Wouldn't hurt you one bit."

There was an edge to the old man's voice that Jake didn't understand. "Support the local artisans?" he said lightly.

"That's one way to put it." Abe hauled himself to his feet. "Gotta go, boy. Nice talkin' to you."

"Thanks, Abe. Good to see you again."

As Abe limped toward the door of his house, Jake set off down the street.

Shaine still lived in Cranberry Cove. She'd brought up three young boys to adulthood and owned a craft shop.

His feet were now carrying him straight toward that shop.

He'd never known that her parents had died.

He'd never asked.

He could turn around right now, and head for the airport. Nothing to stop him and every nerve in his body telling him to put as much distance as he could between himself and any possibility of meeting Shaine O'Sullivan.

Ahead of him, he saw Maggie Stearns climb the steps of her house and go in the front door. When it came to gossip, Abe was a rank amateur compared to Maggie. In no mood to meet her, Jake hurried down the street, and saw a classy carved wooden sign that announced The Fin Whale Craft Shop.

Shaine had always loved whales. When three humpbacks had breached offshore that day on Ghost Island, he'd seen it as a good omen.

Which just went to show how wrong a man could be.

The sign hung over the door; it was swaying gently in the wind. Shaine's intelligence had been one of the many things he'd loved about her, and he had no doubt that she'd make a success of any venture she embarked upon.

He came to a sudden halt in front of the window. Placed on an easel, with a light behind it, was a stained glass panel of a whale breaching, the glass blending blues, greens and all the shades in between, the spray a dazzling white. Jake knew, immediately and instinctively, that it was Shaine's work; and couldn't have said where that knowledge came from, other than that she'd always been artistic.

The panel was very beautiful. He knew people in the Hamptons who'd be happy to have it hanging in one of their windows, and who'd pay good money for the privilege.

He wouldn't mind owning it himself.

He put his hand on the door and walked inside.

In a split second he gained an impression of well-crafted objects displayed to their full advantage. Then his attention flew to the woman standing behind the counter. She was reaching up to put some boxes on the shelves, her back to him. But as she heard the bell tinkle over the door, she half turned. "I'll be right with you…"

Her voice died away. The color fled from her cheeks; the boxes tumbled to the floor. She grabbed for the counter with one hand, swaying on her feet as the sign had swayed in the wind. Her eyes, those green eyes he'd never forgotten, were huge, filled with an emotion he could only call terror. As her hand slipped from the edge of the counter and her eyes rolled up in her head, Jake crossed the floor in four quick strides, pushing aside a chair so he could get behind the counter.

He grabbed her by the waist just before she fell. "It's okay," he said, "I've got you."

She slumped against him, her body boneless, her head

butting his chest. Even though she was slimmer than he remembered, he had to brace himself against her weight. As gently as he could, he lowered her to the chair, easing her head between her legs. Her dress was a vibrant green, with swirls of tropical fish in all hues of the rainbow; Shaine had never been one for sedate colors.

The feel of her skin against his fingers jolted through his body. Had it always been so smooth and silky, creamy like the milk from the Jersey cow his father had owned? Her scent was flowery, subtle and complex without being overpowering; her hair was shot with gold from the overhead light.

Her nape, slender and delicate, aroused in him such a confusion of emotion that again Jake was seized with the urge to run for his life.

He stayed where he was. She made a small sound of distress, her voice muffled. Kneeling beside her, Jake repeated, "It's okay, Shaine, you nearly fainted, that's all."

She'd fainted, he thought, because the sight of him had terrified her. Reluctantly his brain began to work. Why terror? Anger he would have understood. Or disdain. Even just plain indifference after all these years. But terror?

She was pushing her hands against her knees, slowly raising her head; her fingers, nicked with many small white scars, were ringless. No wedding band or engagement ring. Jake said the first thing that came into his mind. "You've cut your hair."

At eighteen, her hair had rippled down her back in unruly waves. Now it hugged her scalp in an aureole of fire, baring the long line of her throat and the fragile bones of her face. She was breathing in shallow gasps. He added urgently, "Take your time, there's no rush."

For the first time she looked right at him. "It is you," she said in a thin voice. "Jake. Jake Reilly."

"I didn't mean to frighten you."

She straightened, easing her spine against the back of the

chair, then pushed away his hand, which had been resting on her thigh. "What are you doing here?"

"I was on business in Montreal, and figured I was close enough to Newfoundland I should come back and see what was going on," he said with an ease that sounded totally fake.

"After thirteen years."

"I wasn't expecting to see you," he said. Abruptly he pushed himself to his feet, needing to put some distance between himself and her. "I thought you'd have left years ago."

"We've nothing to say to each other. And I can't imagine you'd have anything to say to anyone else here, either."

He said with awkward sincerity, "Abe Gamble told me about your parents, Shaine. I'm really sorry."

"It was a long time ago." Fear, stark and unmistakable, flickered in the green depths of her irises. "What else did he tell you?"

"That you came back from university to bring up your brothers. Under any other circumstances, I can't imagine that would have been your choice."

"You know nothing about my circumstances. Or about me," she said inimically.

But Jake had been doing arithmetic in his head. "Connor's out of school, Abe said. He must be, what—eighteen now? So why haven't you left, now that they're all grown up?"

"It's not as easy to get away as you might think," she flashed. "I've sunk all my money into this shop, I can't just pick up like you did and disappear."

"You wouldn't come with me!"

"I did the right thing," she said with a stubborn lift of her chin. A chin that in its very feminine way was every bit as determined as his own.

"I'm glad you have no regrets," he said with a good dose of sarcasm and a total disregard for truth.

Shaine stood up herself, gripping the counter with one hand. Then she looked him up and down with deliberate hauteur. "You don't belong here anymore—you stand out like the rest of the city slickers who come here every summer. Cranberry Cove's not home to you. But it's home to me, and I don't want you here."

"Don't you? Now why would that be?"

"You left here and you never once got in touch," she said bitterly. "Not once. You don't have the right to ask me a single question—you gave up that right years ago."

It was no moment for Jake to discover that all he wanted to do was put his arms around her and kiss her until the turmoil in his chest changed to something straightforward, like lust. "Your face," he said slowly, "it's different. Fined down, as though somehow you've grown into it. It hasn't been easy for you, has it?"

"That's none of your business," she said tightly. "So why don't you just leave? And this time, don't bother coming back."

But Jake wasn't about to be deflected. "You're more beautiful than ever, that's what I'm trying to say."

For a moment, he would have sworn, pleasure glanced off the blazing green of her eyes. "Keep that line for someone else," she flared. "I don't need it."

"There isn't anyone else. I haven't married, or even come close. What about you?"

Her lips, so delectably soft and sensual, thinned. "You just don't get it, do you? Get out of my shop, Jake. Get out of my life. I never want to see you again!"

"You ought to remember something," he said with dangerous softness. "I don't like being told what to do."

"You've never grown up, that's what you mean. Your needs are what's important. Not anyone else's." Her voice hardened. "If you don't leave, I'll call my brothers to come and put you out."

''You'd have to call all three of them,'' he said, laughter bubbling in his chest. ''I don't fight fair.''

''That's the first true word you've said since you walked in that door.''

''Why were you so scared?''

''You took me by surprise, that's all.'' In an agony of impatience she burst out, ''Just go, why don't you?''

''I'm going because I choose to. Not because you're handing out orders right and left.''

''I don't give a damn about your motives!''

Jake wasn't sure he had anything as clear-cut as motives; he felt like a bullet ricocheting from wall to wall. With sudden fierceness he wished he could rewrite this whole meeting. He and Shaine had been friends; and now were glaring at each other as though they were mortal enemies. He said roughly, ''I wish you well, in whatever you do. You have some beautiful things in your shop. The glass panel in the window, for instance—you made that, didn't you?''

''Yes,'' she said grudgingly.

''If no one buys it, get in touch with me.'' He brought out his wallet and dropped one of his cards on the counter. ''I know people who'd pay a lot of money for work like that.''

She didn't even glance at the card. ''I have an agent already,'' she snapped. ''How dare you walk in the door after all these years and think you can fix my life?''

''One thing hasn't changed,'' he said. ''Your temper always did match your hair.''

In a swirl of brightly patterned skirts she pushed past him and stalked toward the door. Opening it, she said, ''Goodbye, Jake. Have a wonderful life.''

He crossed the polished softwood floor, the old boards creaking underfoot. If there was fury in her eyes, there was also something akin to panic. She wanted him gone, and gone now. But he still had no idea why. ''Goodbye,

Shaine,'' he said. Then, before she could evade him, he dropped his hands to her shoulders and kissed her hard on the mouth.

For a moment she was rigid, as though he'd taken her completely by surprise. Then, suddenly, she was quivering like a frightened bird. He pulled her closer, his eyes closed, lost to everything but the softness and warmth of her lips, the fragility of the bones taut under his fingers. The heat from her skin seeped through her dress, warming him in a place so deeply buried he'd all but forgotten it.

He wanted her. God, how he wanted her.

Pulling her to the length of his body, Jake deepened his kiss, letting all his passionate need of her speak for itself. And then realized that she was struggling, twisting away from him, trying desperately to tug her mouth free of his.

Dazed, he raised his head and spoke the first words that came to mind. "That hasn't changed," he said thickly.

"Everything's changed," she spat, flags of color flaring on her cheeks. "Do you honestly think you can walk in the door and pick up as if thirteen years haven't gone by?"

Put like that, it didn't sound too sensible. Still struggling to subdue a reaction that had shocked him with its intensity, Jake muttered, "I hadn't planned on kissing—"

"You're sure not getting the chance again."

The words were out before he could stop them. "You didn't like making love with me on Ghost Island."

Her jaw dropped. "What are you talking about?"

"That's why you wouldn't go away with me—sexually, I failed you in some way."

She said brusquely, "Don't be ridiculous! I loved what we did."

"Is that the truth?" he demanded, and realized how deep it had gone, the certainty that he'd disappointed her. He'd only been twenty-two; and she'd meant the world to him.

"Yes, it's the truth, and I'm not getting into all that— it's too long ago to matter anymore."

"Not to me, it isn't."

"You expect me to believe you?" She shoved the door further open with her hip. "Get out of my life, Jake Reilly. And stay out."

She meant it. She wasn't being coy or playing games; she hadn't had a manipulative bone in her body as a girl or a young woman. Jake turned on his heel, closed the door very carefully behind him and set off down the street.

He had no idea where he was going.

Yes, he did. He was going back to his rented car and driving to the airport just as fast as the car would take him. Which wouldn't be nearly fast enough.

Whether or not she'd liked making love with him that one time, Shaine now hated his guts.

Desire had vanished, eclipsed by what was unquestionably pain. The same pain he'd felt on Ghost Island when Shaine—after they had made heated, inexpert and passionate love, after he'd poured his heart out to her—had said to him, "I can't leave Cranberry Cove with you, Jake. I have to stay here."

She had stayed. He was the one who'd left, left on his own that very day and done his best to forget her.

The day before yesterday he would have said he'd succeeded. But that was when the idea had come to him on a crowded Montreal street to fly to Newfoundland and see Cranberry Cove through the eyes of a grown man.

Bad move. Very bad move. Downright stupid move.

Shaine watched through the window until Jake was out of sight, and realized she was trembling with reaction.

He'd gone. For now.

But would he stay long enough in the cove to discover her secret? And then would he come back?

Again sheer terror coursed through her veins. She

switched the sign in the window from Open to Closed, locked the door, turned off the lights and hurried into the back room. Sinking into a chair, she buried her face in her hands.

CHAPTER TWO

WITHOUT making a conscious choice, Jake realized he was walking toward the high school where he'd been the captain of the hockey team and a local hero. He slowed down. It all seemed such a long time ago: the bite of his skates into the ice; the blur of the puck as it whipped into the net; the screaming fans; and, of course, the adoring girls in his class. What did it all mean now? He hadn't played hockey for years; he'd been too busy amassing his fortune and building a carefully selected, international clientele.

Some boys were playing basketball in the yard to one side of the school, where a net had been screwed to the brick wall and white lines painted on the pavement. Jake had played there himself many times, keeping fit all summer until hockey began again in the fall. Absently he watched, glad of the distraction.

One boy stood out from the rest for the speed of his reactions and the accuracy of his shots; Jake's attention sharpened. The boy was skinny, outstripping his height, and almost danced with the ball, so that it became an extension of his fingertips; the others circled him, trying to distract him, only occasionally deflecting the pure arc of the ball against the brick wall, the swish as it fell through the metal circle of the net. But it was all in fun. The shouts were good-natured, and as often as not the boy would bounce the ball to one of his companions, letting him have a chance at the net, as comfortable with a defensive position as with an offensive.

Nice kid, Jake thought, noting the boy's thatch of dark hair and wide grin. He'd make a good hockey player. Although he looked too young for high school.

What would become of him? Would he be content to stay in the village and follow in the footsteps of his father, fishing for crab and lobster in the dangerous waters off-shore? Or would he seek wider horizons, and grow away from the place that had birthed him?

Restlessly Jake moved his shoulders under his leather jacket. It wasn't like him to be fanciful, or to involve himself too deeply in the lives of others. So why was he mooning over the future of a kid who meant nothing to him?

Then the boy neatly nipped the ball from one of the other players, zigzagged through a defensive line that had been caught off guard, and leaped high in the air, his body and the ball one elegant, continuous curve. As the ball sank through the net, Jake had to conquer the impulse to applaud.

Couldn't he find something better to do than clap for a kid he didn't even know? Turning away, getting his bearings, Jake set off toward the street where he'd parked his car. He'd made his choices many years ago and there was no going back. He should never have come here. Although he was doing his best to ignore it, there was a cold lump in the pit of his stomach, and it would take very little to replay the scene in Shaine's shop. If he'd known she was still living here, he wouldn't have come near the place. Because that choice, too, had been made years ago: by her, initially, and then by him.

He strode along the street, head down, wanting nothing more than to be in his car and on the road south. His private jet was at the Deer Lake airport. Assuming the weather held, he could leave tonight.

"Well, if it isn't Jake Reilly."

Jake looked up, and for a moment couldn't place the man standing in front of him, hands on his hips, the look on his face far from friendly. "Padric," Jake said slowly. The last time he'd seen Shaine's brothers, Padric had been a stringy eight-year-old; he'd grown into a tall, rugged young man with a mop of curly chestnut hair and opaque gray eyes.

"I heard you were in these parts," Padric drawled. "Local boy makes good and comes back to his roots—you've been watching too much TV."

"So you're no happier to see me than Shaine was."

"Where'd you see Shaine?" Padric rapped.

"In her store. Why?"

"Headed right for her, did you?"

"Cranberry Cove's not big enough to avoid her," Jake said with partial truth.

"You're about as welcome around here as a sculpin in a drag net—I bet she gave you the same message."

"A little more subtly than you."

Padric's voice was laden with sarcasm. "We all really appreciated the sympathy card you sent when our parents died."

Jake met his gaze unflinchingly. "I didn't know they'd died until I bumped into Abe today."

"Right. Couldn't wait to shake the dust of the cove off your boots all those years ago. You've never looked back, have you?"

"I had other things on my mind."

"Like making money. You don't belong here anymore, buddy. So why don't you hike right back to the big city and forget about us country bumpkins?"

"You're acting like I committed a crime by leaving the village," Jake said forcibly. "I went to university when I was seventeen, came back at twenty-two when my dad drowned, and left again once my mum went to Australia. Nothing wrong with any of that, Padric."

"You were Shaine's friend. Or that's what we thought. Guess we were wrong, though."

"Don't speculate about stuff you know nothing about!"

"Get off my case," Padric said softly.

Although he could tell Padric was spoiling for a fight, it

wasn't in Jake's plans to start a street brawl with one of Shaine's brothers. He said flatly, "I'm on my way back to my car to get out of here for the third time. So back off."

Briefly, relief was as unmistakably stamped on Padric's face as terror had been on Shaine's. Nor, Jake decided, was it relief that Padric was being spared a fight; Padric had always been a boy to use his fists first and think afterward. What the devil was going on?

"You do that," Padric said. "Unless you want to find yourself flat on your back in the ditch."

It would have been all too easy to respond in kind, because Jake was still smarting from Shaine's harshness: Padric's posturing on top of that was the last thing he needed. But Jake had learned in city boardrooms to pick his fights, and this wasn't one he intended to engage. He said evenly, "Ask Shaine why I left the second time—you might be surprised by the answer." With an edge of real emotion, he heard himself add, "Take care of her, Padric."

"We all do. Devlin, me and Connor. We don't need you putting your oar in."

Feeling his temper rise in spite of himself, Jake pushed past the other man and crossed the street. He could already see his car. Thank heaven for small mercies, he thought dryly, and a few moments later was inserting his key into the ignition. Signaling, he pulled out into the street and turned toward Breakheart Hill.

Where Shaine's parents had died in an accident.

He wasn't going to think about Shaine.

The rental car was as different from his Ferrari as a car could be; it labored up the hill, giving Jake lots of time to watch the cove recede in his rearview mirror. Why had both Shaine and Padric been intent on him leaving the village the same day he'd arrived? Why had she been so afraid, and Padric so belligerent?

Did he want the answer to those questions? Or did he

indeed want to shake the dust of Cranberry Cove off his expensive Italian loafers?

Seven miles down the road, in the next village, was a small motel and restaurant. Jake pulled in, and for several minutes sat drumming his fingers on the wheel. Back to Manhattan or back to Cranberry Cove. His choice.

He hadn't had anything to eat since breakfast early that morning; so in the end it was his stomach that decided for him. Half an hour later, he had a room for the night and was tucking into an excellent seafood platter in the little restaurant.

He wouldn't go back to the cove tonight. He'd let both Shaine and Padric think he was gone for good. Then tomorrow he'd confront Shaine again.

Kiss her again? And this time see if he could make her respond? Was that the real reason he wasn't on his jet bound for New York?

In the morning Jake wasn't so sure about going back to the cove. Why meddle where he wasn't wanted and risk another rejection? His skin wasn't that thick. In fact, he thought acerbically, where Shaine was concerned, it was distressingly thin.

Perhaps she'd had a lover hidden in a back room, and that explained her terror. Or she was engaged to be married, despite her lack of ring, and didn't want her past surfacing in the form of Jake Reilly.

How many lovers had she had in the last thirteen years? There'd be no lack of men pursuing her; her sensuality, intelligence and sheer beauty would see to that.

He glanced at the clock. It always used to be Shaine's habit to start her day by jogging around the lake just east of the village. He could be there in fifteen minutes. And if she didn't turn up, nobody would be any the wiser.

It took Jake fourteen minutes to get to the parking lot by the lakeshore. Although there were no other cars, he knew

Shaine could easily jog here from home. He stretched against the sturdy wooden fence around the changing rooms, the breeze pleasantly cool against his bare legs. Seeking out breaks in the trees that would reveal anyone on the trail, he let his eyes follow the shoreline all around the lake. And then he saw her. She was just rounding the curve of the lake that was nearest the highway, moving easily, her red hair like a beacon.

Hidden by the undergrowth, he set off toward her at a slow run, wondering when she'd see him and what she'd do when she did. It wouldn't be predictable and it almost certainly wouldn't be cool, calm and collected. Round two, he thought with a tingle of anticipation, speeding up. She'd won the first round. But if he had his way, she wouldn't win the second.

A grove of birches, their leaves already tinged with gold, concealed the last stretch of shoreline. Then he spurted around a corner, his steps deadened by the grass, and almost collided with her head-on. She stopped dead in her tracks, her breasts heaving.

Her first reaction was fear. But this time the fear was rapidly overtaken by fury. With unholy amusement Jake watched her eyes spark like emeralds and her chin snap up. She said with dangerous calm, "You told Padric you were leaving."

"I changed my mind."

"And you just happened to be jogging around the lake at the same time as me? What's with you, Jake? Have you got spies all over the village?"

"You used to jog here years ago."

"Oh," she said with saccharine sweetness, "so you actually remember something about me—how flattering."

He said with raw truth, "I doubt I've ever forgotten anything about you."

"Don't feed me that garbage—it might work on your fancy city women, but it doesn't cut any ice with me."

"I've never fed you a line in my life, and I'm not about to start now."

"The sad thing is that I almost believe you," she said. "That's pretty pathetic, isn't it?"

"Do we have to fight, Shaine? We were friends once. Good friends."

"Yes. And then we made love and wrecked a friendship that meant all the world to me."

"You'd promised all along—way before we made love—that you'd leave the cove with me. But when push came to shove, you wouldn't do it."

"I changed my mind," she retorted. "Or is that just a male prerogative?"

"You didn't love me enough—that's what you said."

"And that's what I meant."

Even now, her words had the power to hurt. "You lied to—what's that noise?"

The alders behind Shaine had started shaking, as though a very large animal was moving through them. Overpowering the gentle splash of waves on the sand, Jake heard the crack of branches, and the thick rustle of dried ferns. Shaine looked back over her shoulder. Into the clearing stepped a magnificent bull moose with a full rack of antlers, his long dewlap dangling below his chin, his Roman nose testing the air. With his front leg, he pawed the ground. Clumps of dirt arched backward, hitting the ground with dull thuds.

This was September. Rutting season. Jake said tersely, "Back up, Shaine. Toward me."

She did exactly as he'd asked. Under her breath she muttered, "Shouldn't we be climbing a tree?"

"Birch trees are beautiful, but they wouldn't hold your weight, let alone mine. Keep moving slowly, no sudden moves, that's it."

He, too, was backing away. While a moose, bull or cow, looked like one of creation's jokes, as though it had been made up of leftover parts from several other animals, Jake also knew that a male in rut was nothing to laugh about. As though proving his point, the moose struck his huge antlers against the trunk of the nearest birch, uttering guttural grunts as he did so. The tree shuddered from the force of the blow.

"We'll be out of sight in a few moments," Jake whispered. "Then we'll run as fast as we can for the fence."

"Not sure I can run," she muttered. "My knees are as wobbly as that birch tree."

The bull took three steps toward them, shaking its rack from side to side. Then, as Jake and Shaine kept backing up, the shower of golden leaves hid it from view. "Okay," Jake said, "run!"

She took off like a bullet out of a gun, with him hard on her heels. Ears straining, he heard the bull grunt again. Then, to his dismay, he heard hooves strike the ground at a fast trot, thudding along the path behind him. "Faster!" he yelled. "We'll have to jump the fence, we'll be safe inside."

When Shaine reached the painted wooden fence around the changing rooms, Jake lifted her bodily from behind and heaved her over the top. Risking a glance over his shoulder, he saw the moose had speeded to a canter; it was scarcely twenty feet from him. With an agility he hadn't known he possessed, he leaped for the top of the fence, felt something scrape his back and tumbled over to the other side. His shoulder hit the grass hard, driving the air from his lungs. As the bull butted the fence with bruising strength, the wood groaned like a creature in pain.

From behind the alders, where the swamp lay, came the long-drawn-out bellow of a female moose in heat.

Jake pushed himself partway up, his heart racketing in his chest. Through the narrow slats in the fence he saw the moose raise his head, his softly furred ears angled toward the swamp, breath puffing from his nostrils. As calmly as if he'd never pounded after them along the trail, the animal trotted away, his great hump dark against the yellow leaves and silver branches of the birches. Within moments he was out of sight. Jake leaned back against the fence and began to laugh.

"That wasn't funny!" Shaine protested. "He could have killed us."

"The look on your face when you saw him," Jake gasped, "it was priceless."

A reluctant smile tugged at her lips. "What about the look on your face when you came over the fence?"

"I could hear the damn thing breathing down my neck—it was no time for dignity."

She giggled. "Have you ever considered the Olympics? That was a gold medal jump."

"Hey, what about the 25-meter dash—we're naturals."

By now she was laughing as helplessly as he. "Where's a stopwatch when you need it? We broke a world record and there was no one here to time it."

"I'm just as glad we didn't have an audience. I'd never live that one down in the boardroom."

Her face changed. "Jake, he tore your shirt. Oh Jake, there's blood!"

"Don't fuss," Jake said, his mouth still split in a big grin, "it's only a graze. We're lucky we didn't get our behinds full of splinters."

But Shaine was on her knees beside him, the concern in her face making his heart turn over in his chest. "You'd better see a doctor—have you had a tetanus shot lately? It needs washing and a good dollop of antiseptic."

Yesterday, when he'd turned up in her shop, she'd acted as though a small wound would be the very least she'd wish on him. But now her fingers were cool on his flesh, making ripples of sensation spread the width of his shoulders and down his torso. He shifted, took her in his arms, and kissed her.

Because she was off balance on the ground, she clung to him, a move that brought her breasts in their thin T-shirt against his rib cage. He'd never forgotten her breasts, either, he thought dimly, so firm and delectable, so sweetly pointed. Teasing her lips apart, he drove into her with his tongue, heard her moan deep in her throat, and pushed her back into the grass. She tasted of salt and herbal soap.

To his utter amazement he realized she was gripping him fiercely by the shoulders, her mouth open and hungry, her tongue twined with his. Desire surged through his veins. He lowered his hips to hers, his arousal instant and imperative; and felt her move beneath him with an ardor that made the blood sing through his limbs. He rolled over, pulling her with him, wrapping his thighs around her long bare legs. His hands roamed her body, finding the rippled rib cage, the sweet curve of one hip, then searching out the rise of her breast, its tip hard as a pebble.

She gasped his name, digging her fingers into his scalp to draw his head lower. His tongue laved the line of her throat, then found the pulse thrumming in the little hollow at its base. Had he needed any proof that she was as desperate for him as he for her, he had it there. But did he need proof, when she was kissing his forehead, his cheekbones, his lips like a woman who'd never kissed a man before?

Length to length and heat to heat. This was why he'd come back.

Jake tugged at her brief T-shirt, slid one hand below it, and pulled her bra down so he could caress her nipple with his fingers. Shuddering in his arms, Shaine lifted her hips to press them into his, rubbing against him in a way calculated to drive him insane. "Shaine," he muttered, his whole body suffused with an agony of longing. "Oh God, Shaine, I've never forgotten anything about you."

"Neither have—" Shaine stopped abruptly, in midsentence; her own words sounded like those of a stranger. A woman she didn't know. With all her strength she pushed Jake away and sat up. "What am I *doing?*" she cried. Her hands shaking, she tried to thrust her shirt back into the waistband of her shorts.

Jake also sat up, taking her by the shoulders. "You were doing what you wanted to do," he said forcefully. "Don't you remember what it was like on the island? We fell on each other, it was as though we were made for each other—you can't have forgotten that."

She twisted away from him and scrambled to her feet. As Jake got up, too, she said furiously, "I don't know who I'm angrier with, you or me. Me, I guess. All you had to do was look at me and I fell flat on my back. Kissing you like I was eighteen again. Moaning and writhing like someone demented. I'd have made love with you on the grass in a public park!"

Jake held his tongue. He'd always had a healthy respect for Shaine's temper, learning a long time ago that trying to stem it was a lost cause. Without a pause for breath she seethed, "I'm no better than that cow moose, caterwauling in the swamp. Come and get me, I'm yours. Dammit, Jake Reilly, why did you have to come back? I was doing just fine without you. So what if I've been living like a nun for years, there's nothing wrong with celibacy because men are jerks—and in that particular category you take the gold medal. No contest. Anyway, you said you were leaving last night. More of your lies are exactly what I don't need and why don't you say something?"

"I was waiting until you shut up," Jake said, trying very hard to keep his gaze on her face rather than her heaving breasts.

Her eyes narrowed. "The last thing I need is you back in my life. I don't want to go to bed with anyone and you top the list."

Reprehensibly, Jake discovered he was enjoying himself.

"That's not the message I was getting. And do you know what, Shaine? I haven't laughed like that in years."

"Neither have I and so what?"

He gave her a lazy grin. "You're pretty damn cute when you lose your temper."

"Save your compliments for someone who cares."

"You're also the most beautiful woman I've ever seen, and I've seen a few."

"I bet you have. And I bet they fall all over you. Just like me."

"No," he said. "Not like you. You're unique. You always were."

"Everyone's unique," she retorted. "Or have you been too busy making money to figure that out yet?"

"Then you're more unique than the rest," he drawled. "And there's nothing wrong with making money."

"Providing you don't sell your soul in the process."

His jaw tightened. "Are you accusing me of that?"

"What do you think?"

Suddenly, it was no longer a game. "That you don't know what you're talking about."

"I beg to differ." She lifted her chin, the light glinting in the green depths of her eyes, and with fierce intensity said, "Go back where you belong. Today. Now. And leave me alone. I've built a good life here and I value it…I don't want you or anyone else wrecking it because every now and then my hormones get out of hand."

"How many years of celibacy are we talking?" he asked with very real curiosity. The answer mattered to him. It shouldn't, but it did.

"That's my business."

"So all men are jerks?"

"That's what I said."

"Then you couldn't have done a very good job bringing up your brothers."

"They're the exceptions that prove the rule." She bit her

lip, her temper dying. "Don't amuse yourself at my expense, that's what I'm saying. You never used to be cruel, Jake…don't start now. Not with me."

The vulnerable curve of her mouth smote him to the heart. She was right to chastise him, Jake thought. He had no idea how she'd spent the last thirteen years, and no right to ask. The reason being that he'd turned his back on the cove and on her and hadn't once allowed himself to look back. His choice. To which there were consequences.

It had taken a beautiful red-haired woman standing in the early morning sunlight to make him feel the loss of those years. The hollow they'd left in his heart and his soul.

She said flatly, glancing at her watch, "I've got to go, I'm opening the shop this morning. Take care of yourself, won't you? You did the right thing to leave here—the cove was never big enough for you."

Then she turned on her heel, walked steadily toward the gate, opened it in a squeal of hinges, closed it behind her and started to jog away from him.

Like a man who'd been hit on the head—or chased by a bull moose—Jake stood still. His limbs felt heavy, too heavy to move. His heart, he thought, felt heavier still.

Why had he never gotten in touch with Shaine even once in the thirteen years since he'd last left the cove?

Hurt, he thought. The pain of realizing that the young woman to whom he'd given his heart had spurned him; that she didn't love him enough to trust in a future with him. Humiliation, because he'd been afraid he hadn't measured up sexually. Pride, following fast on the heels of humiliation. Pride or sheer cussedness. The label didn't matter. And then, of course, work. He'd submerged himself in his own ambitions, in his drive to separate himself from the place where he'd grown up and to make his mark on the world. A world of major players, where every move counted, and every decision was watched.

He'd succeeded. Through a combination of mathematical

smarts, persistence and fourteen-hour days, he'd smashed through the barriers that should have kept a man from Cranberry Cove out of the big leagues. He'd made it.

But, Jake wondered, at what cost? One thing was obvious. He'd lost any pretensions to the long-ago friendship he'd shared with Shaine as she grew from adolescence into young womanhood. So what was left? Lust?

Even the thoughts of her hands on him, her tongue laced with his, were enough to stir his body to life again. He swore under his breath. She'd been infuriated by her body's betrayal. And why wouldn't it betray her if she'd been living like a nun?

Shaine, according to her, had been celibate for years. So had her reaction at the first sight of him been a fear of abandoning that celibacy?

Jake had a very clear understanding that women found him attractive; it had been proven often enough. But he wasn't vain enough to think that one look at him had driven Shaine mad with passion and then caused her to faint dead away. No, that theory wouldn't wash.

He wandered back to his car, another uncomfortable insight nudging his consciousness. He could be a stiff-necked SOB when he wanted to be, a trait that had stood him in good stead during those times when he'd thought he couldn't possibly force his way into the corridors of power. Had there been, behind his ferocious ambitions, an element of *I'll show her what I can do*…as if Shaine cared how much money he made.

Although, he thought wryly, he'd be willing to bet she'd love his silver Ferrari.

She'd made a life without him and didn't want him upsetting it. That was the basic message.

Was he going to respect it? Drive away from the motel in the opposite direction to Cranberry Cove, that part of his life from now on a closed book?

Not once, in the thirteen years since he'd seen her, had

he desired a woman as he desired Shaine. That much he'd learned in the last two days. He'd had affairs, of course he had. Enjoyed them while they lasted, ended them with no regrets and no nagging sense that he should commit himself, or—heaven forbid—get married.

Shaine was different. She always had been.

Did he want to marry Shaine? Surely not!

But maybe he needed her, he thought slowly. Her temper, her laughter and her passion...

Like a man surfacing from a dream, Jake looked around. The birch leaves were still a shimmer of sunshine yellow, but Shaine was nowhere in sight. He drove back to the motel, showered and put a rough bandage on the scrape on his back. Then he had a late breakfast of bacon, eggs and hash browns, no doubt bad for him but very tasty. As he drained his third cup of bracingly hot coffee, he realized he'd come to a decision. Once again, he was going back to the cove. He had no idea what he was going to do when he got there. But he couldn't just turn tail and run for home.

He'd run away all those years ago. Once was enough.

CHAPTER THREE

Two hours later, Jake was parking his car outside the rink in Cranberry Cove. His campaign—a word that seemed to suit his state of mind—might as well start here as anywhere. Maybe revisiting the site of so many of his adolescent triumphs would help him plan a course of action. Short of walking into The Fin Whale Craft Shop and buying the stained-glass panel, he was distressingly short of anything else that could be called a plan.

It was Saturday. There was bound to be a practice session going on, if not a game.

The arena smelled of cold, trapped air, sweaty hockey gear and damp wooden floors, and took him back in time as though he was sixteen again, a gangly teenager who'd yet to fill out to fit his height. Two teams were doing drills, the coaches barking orders, their whistles shrilling; and that, too, filled him with nostalgia. Sticks slapped the ice. The steel blades of the players' skates whined and rasped as they carved into the surface of the rink.

Peewee league, thought Jake. Ages eleven to twelve. With keen interest he watched the players, amused by their blunders, impressed by their expertise. Then his eyes sharpened. Surely that tall kid who'd just whipped the puck from his opponent in one smooth stroke was the same one he'd seen playing basketball at the school? The identical lightning-swift reactions, the unmistakable grace and pleasure in what he was doing. So he could skate, that kid. Skate extraordinarily well.

Tucked at one end of the bleachers, Jake followed all the well-known moves. When he got back to Manhattan, he was going to find an amateur league and start playing again, he vowed to himself. Even now, he could feel the old ache to tie on a pair of skates and join the fast-moving figures on the ice.

The boy was good. But he, Jake, could show him a trick or two.

He hadn't yet had a good look at the boy's face, because all the players were wearing plastic helmets and protective masks. Then the whistles blew once again, and the skaters trooped off the ice. On the bench they hauled on regulation sweaters, one team's dark blue, the other's white and black. Five players from each team took their positions on the ice, the heavily padded goalies doing stretches in front of the nets. Jake shifted along the bleachers so he was nearer to the center line. The boy he was interested in was playing offense, waiting for the face-off.

He played like a pro, weaving in and out of the other players, passing the puck to his teammates with demonic accuracy and firing shots on goal with a flare Jake could only admire. One thing stood out. He loved the game. Loved it as Jake had loved it.

Swamped with memories, Jake heard the whistle blow for a change-over of players. The boy skated away from Jake, and for the first time Jake took a moment to read the white letters on the back of his sweater. O'Sullivan, they said.

The boy's last name was O'Sullivan?

Jake frowned. The kid was too old to be Devlin's son, and far too young to be Connor. He must have borrowed someone else's sweater.

There were no other O'Sullivans in the cove. Shaine's father had been the only one, their nearest relatives living on the other side of Newfoundland, in St. John's.

Then the boy hauled off his helmet, his sweat-soaked hair flattened to his skull, and turned to the coach, saying something that made the man laugh. The boy had dark hair, dark as Jake's, and eyes blue as his sweater.

All the O'Sullivans had red hair, and eyes that were either green like Shaine's or gray like Padric's.

Jake's hands were ice-cold, and there was a lump of ice lodged in his belly. As if he'd never won the provincial medal in mathematics, his analytical mind fumbled with the arithmetic. He himself had left the cove thirteen years ago, right after making love with Shaine. The boy looked to be about twelve years old.

No, thought Jake. No.

The boy couldn't be his son. Couldn't be.

The other branch of the O'Sullivan family must have moved to the cove. That was it. The boy was Shaine's first cousin.

If they'd moved, Abe would have told him about it. Abe, Jake remembered sickly, had said a couple of very pointed things about men who stayed away from their home turf for too long, and found a surprise or two when they came back. What else had Abe said? *There's things keep a woman home*. Had Shaine stayed in Cranberry Cove because he, Jake, had left her pregnant?

Was that why she'd looked so terrified when he'd walked into her shop without any warning? If Jake was the father of her son, of course she'd have been terrified. Of course she'd insisted he leave the cove that very day. She hadn't wanted him finding out her secret.

She'd never told him he had a son. Not twelve years ago, and not yesterday.

Jake leaned forward, filling his lungs with cold air and exhaling slowly. Take it easy, he told himself, quit jumping to conclusions. So the kid's an extremely good hockey player, and he has dark hair and blue eyes. Lots of kids have dark hair and blue eyes. Your imagination's in overdrive.

If the boy on the bench was his son, it would explain Padric's hostility. It would even explain Shaine's self-imposed celibacy. What chance would she have for affairs if she was living with her young son in a small village where everyone knew everyone else's business?

Everything fit.

He, Jake Reilly, was the father of a twelve-year-old son.

Jake let the words circle in his brain, trying to bridge the enormous gap between the man who'd walked into the rink thirty minutes ago, and the man who was now sitting on the bench staring down at his hands, which were white-knuckled with strain.

Shaine had never told him he'd fathered a child. She could have. He hadn't exactly had a low profile the last few years. It would have taken only a few minutes' research on the Internet to find out his business address.

The conclusion was inescapable. She hadn't wanted him to know.

His throat was dry, his heart pounding as though he was the one who'd been skating back and forth from one end of the rink to the other. Then, to his utter consternation, as he glanced over at the bench again, the boy looked his way. Blue eyes locked with blue eyes, and held.

Jake could no more have looked away than he could have flown out the door. The boy's grin froze in place, his padded shoulders held at an awkward angle, unmoving, as if he were a deer trapped in the beam of the poacher's light. Then the coach tapped him on the sleeve; when the boy totally disregarded the signal, the coach tossed out an impatient order. The boy wrenched his head away from Jake's gaze, picked up his helmet and jammed it on his head. It took him several seconds to fasten the strap under his chin.

Grabbing his stick, he pushed open the gate and swung onto the ice. As soon as his back was turned, Jake got up and walked out of the rink, oblivious to anything but the need to be outside where he could breathe.

He didn't even know the boy's first name. His son's name.

His son.

Jake got in his car and drove straight to the craft shop, his hands clamped tightly to the wheel. He parked outside and strode in the door, the little bell jingling in his ears. The young girl behind the counter said politely, "Good morning."

So it was still morning? Jake thought crazily. A morning that seemed to have gone on forever. He'd been chased by a moose, he'd laughed until his sides had hurt and then he'd kissed a beautiful woman until his whole body had been nothing but an explosion of desire.

That woman was the mother of his son. He said roughly, "I'm looking for Shaine."

"She took an early lunch break...she'll be back around one-thirty."

"I know where she lives, I'll find her there," Jake said. "Thanks."

It took all of five minutes to walk to the yellow-painted house at the edge of the cliffs. But when he knocked on the door, no one answered. He pushed the door open and went inside. The back porch was cluttered with coats, shoes and boots. Two sizes of shoes, smaller women's shoes that must belong to Shaine, and much larger ones: sneakers and steel-toed boots, scuffed and undeniably masculine. A boy's jacket was carelessly hung over one of the hooks. In one corner was a heap of old hockey gear and a broken stick.

If he'd needed proof, he had it. "Shaine?" Jake called, his voice dragged from his throat with a huge effort.

The silence was that of an empty house. He marched into the kitchen. Someone, recently, had made sandwiches. The kettle was still hot on the stove. But there was no sign of Shaine.

Attached to the refrigerator door was a photograph of a young boy. Jake walked closer, his eyes glued to the colored image. The boy's hair was as dark as his own, the eyes as blue and as deep-set. But the shape of the face was somehow Shaine's; that, and the tilt of his chin.

Abruptly Jake sat down on the edge of the table. His son was a good-looking boy, humor lurking behind dark lashes, his mouth with a sensitivity that made Jake feel suddenly, overwhelmingly, protective. He knew, as well as any, how life could buffet a man's gentler feelings, sending them underground. He didn't want that for his son.

He still didn't know the boy's name.

He could have gone upstairs to find the right bedroom, and done something as simple as opening one of his son's schoolbooks. But that could wait. First, he had to find Shaine.

Shaine would tell him the name of their son. By God, she would.

The cliff path, he thought. If she had half an hour away from the shop for lunch, and the sun was shining, he'd be willing to bet that's where he'd find her. It was where she'd always gone when she was troubled as a young girl; he could remember her describing how the far horizon, the jut of Ghost Island and the lazy tumble of surf could soothe away her problems.

The last two days, he'd have been a problem. For sure.

He went outside again. Sheets were billowing on the clothesline, white as sails in the wind. Instantly he was catapulted back in time until he was twenty-two again. He'd walked from his house to Shaine's to see if she wanted to drive into Corner Brook that evening to a movie...

Shaine was pegging sheets to the line, her body in its blue dress a lissome curve as the wind-filled cotton fought to be free. She hadn't seen him. Jake stood still in the tall grass, all his senses focused on the young woman at the clothesline. He was in love with her, he thought dazedly. He loved Shaine O'Sullivan with all his heart.

Then she turned and saw him. He moved forward to help her with the wet, white folds of the sheets; when the last one was snapping in the breeze, he took her face in his hands, looked deep into her eyes and said the words that came newly minted to his tongue. "I love you, Shaine."

In her green eyes incredulity was lost in a blaze of joy. She dropped the bag of pegs on the grass and threw her arms around him. "I love you, too—I have for years. Oh, Jake, I'm so happy…"

But she hadn't really meant it. Or if she had, it hadn't been the bone-deep, all-encompassing love that had overwhelmed Jake that sunny spring day.

The long grass rustled its waves of green. Out by Ghost Island a fishing boat idled, the grumble of its motor carrying clearly over the deep blue water. For a moment Jake stood still. Could his property in the Hamptons match this for sheer grandeur? Yet the cove's undeniable beauty had never been enough to hold him here.

He started walking away from the cluster of houses, the grass springy underfoot, gulls mewling overhead, white-breasted as the surf. His dearly loved father had drowned off Ghost Island, in the worst storm in twenty years. His mother, heartbroken, had soon afterward left the village to visit relatives in Australia, and had settled there. Two years later, she'd met Henry Sarton, whom she'd eventually married. Jake liked his stepfather, and could see that his mother was happy again. But, to this day, she'd never once returned to the cove where her first husband had lost his life within sight of the land.

Jake quickened his pace. The spruce trees, stunted by the onshore winds, grew bent to the ground, their boughs densely tangled. Harebells mingled with purple asters and goldenrod in the thick grass, the blossoms brushing against his legs. Crickets chirped, and a fat bumblebee hovered over some late brier roses. Then he saw Shaine.

She was standing by a cluster of rocks near the edge of the cliff, her red hair like a burst of flame. Briefly Jake stood still, feeling anger gather like a whirlwind in his chest. He had no idea what he was going to say to her, or how she would respond. But he did know one thing. It was past time for the truth to come out.

He started walking again, rapidly closing the distance between them.

From the corner of her eye, Shaine caught movement. Her head swung around. Jake was striding toward her along the path, his lean body in faded, snug-fitting jeans and an open-necked shirt both achingly familiar and that of a stranger. He was as graceful as the cougar she'd seen six years ago in the Long Range Mountains; and just as dangerous.

Hadn't she sensed that he would stay? If only she hadn't kissed him this morning with all the pent-up passion of years…what a fool she'd been.

Her heart lurched in her breast. He was closer now; it didn't take much discernment to see he was in a towering rage. He knew, she thought sickly. Every line of his body told her he'd found out about Daniel.

It didn't matter how. What mattered was how she handled it. Taking a deep breath of clean salt air, she braced herself.

To Jake, her body language was all too easily read. You'd better be ready, he thought grimly, because nothing in the world is going to stop me from having my say.

He came to a halt only three feet away from her. She was wearing the same bright dress as the day before, the ocean breeze molding the skirt to her thighs. He said flatly, "I went to the rink. Just for old times' sake."

"So you know," she whispered, and briefly closed her eyes.

"I have a son, don't I? A twelve-year-old son."

"That's right," she said steadily, looking him full in the face.

"That's why you fainted. Why you wanted me to leave yesterday. So I wouldn't find out." Jake seized her by the shoulders, aware at some level that she flinched from his grasp. "You didn't have the guts to tell me. Did you think I wouldn't care?"

"You made love with me on the island all those years ago without any protection. But it never occurred to you to get in touch with me afterward," she said, anger rising like bile in her throat. "So why would I assume you'd care?"

"You told me at the time you were in the safest part of your cycle. Or have you conveniently forgotten that?"

"The world's full of babies conceived that way," she flashed. "You left here and dropped me as if I didn't exist."

"You didn't love me. You said you did that day at the clothesline—but you were lying."

"If you loved me," she said in a low voice, "you had a funny way of showing it."

His grip tightened. "I don't even know my son's name," he said harshly.

"Daniel. We never call him Dan. Although his friends do."

"Daniel O'Sullivan," Jake repeated softly. He liked the sound of it on his tongue. "For God's sake, Shaine," he burst out, "why didn't you get in touch with me?"

The reasons were far too complicated. Nor did he deserve to hear them. "What does it matter? I didn't."

"It matters to me." His voice raw with suppressed feeling, Jake said, "It was like watching a replay of myself on the rink, he even has some of the same moves. The kid's a natural. Just like I was."

"You left here and you never came back," she said implacably. "Never even sent me a Christmas card, never cared enough to find out my parents had died."

Jake spoke the simple truth. "I was hurting too much to get in touch."

Her lashes flickered. Raising her chin, she said, "I brought Daniel up on my own with the help of my three brothers. He's turned out just fine."

"Are you saying he doesn't need me?"

"I guess I am, yes."

"You sure know how to hurt a guy, don't you? I'm his *father,* Shaine. Hasn't he ever asked who his father was?"

"Of course he has," she said shortly.

"What did you tell him?"

"I told him you'd left the cove before I realized I was pregnant. That you knew nothing about him."

"And that's been enough? He hasn't even wanted to know my name?"

"Stop it!" she cried, twisting against his grip. "Let go, you're hurting me."

"You're not going anywhere until we have this out," Jake said curtly. "So Daniel doesn't know who I am."

"You don't belong here anymore! What good would it do him to know your name? I've read about you in those glossy financial magazines. You're a high-flyer, a sophisticated, successful man with houses in New York and Paris, expensive cars, fancy women on your arm and in your bed, too, no doubt. You're as different from us as night from day."

"That's just surface stuff."

"No, it's not—because you won't stay here, Jake. Your real life is somewhere else. Big cities, glamorous hotels, high-powered meetings. You're not going to hang around a rink in Cranberry Cove watching your son play hockey."

"My roots are here!"

"You tore up those roots thirteen years ago. They're dead now. Once roots are dead, you can't replant them."

"I already have. When I kissed you this morning."

"Leave me out of this," she snapped.

"How can I?" Insensibly, Jake's hands gentled on her shoulders. "You're too thin," he said. "You work too hard."

"Stop feeling sorry for me."

She looked as volatile as a cornered raccoon; and about as trustworthy. "What I'm just starting to understand is that your pregnancy and the loss of your parents must have come close together," he said. "I'm so sorry that you were left alone like that. But you could have gotten in touch with me if you'd tried. You could have traced me."

He was right, she probably could have. But at the time there'd been very good reasons why she'd chosen not to. And then the months and years had passed inexorably, all without any word from him, until her decision had hardened into an accustomed way of life. Desperate to deflect him, she said defiantly, "Why would I bother tracing you?"

"Come on, Shaine, you're not a stupid woman. You're the mother of my child—that's why."

"Daniel's mine," she said fiercely, tossing her head so that her silky curls glistened.

A muscle twitched in Jake's jaw. "Are you going to tell him? Or am I?"

"Tell him what?"

He tamped down a rage so strong that it frightened him. "Tell him I'm his father—what else?"

This time Shaine did pull free. Burying her hands in her skirt pockets, fear overcoming any vestige of reason, she said, "Neither one of us is going to tell him anything."

"You'd rather he found out from someone at the rink? Someone who doesn't give a damn about his feelings?"

"He doesn't have to know at all!"

Jake felt as though she'd punched him hard in the gut. "Of course he does."

"No, he doesn't. You didn't speak to him today, did

you? If you had, you'd have found out his name. He doesn't know who you are and that's the way it's going to stay."

Jake took a physical step away from her, a red fog of rage obscuring his vision. Breathing hard, he grated, "You couldn't be more wrong. Who do you think you are? Someone who can turn the clock back? Who can pretend I never turned up here, and that I'm still as ignorant of what happened as I've been all along? Grow up—life doesn't work that way. I know about Daniel. And nothing you can do or say will keep me away from him."

"So what are you going to do? Hire a pack of high-powered lawyers and take him away from me?" Underneath everything else, wasn't that what she was most afraid of?

Once again, Jake thought, she'd gotten past his guard and hit him where he was most vulnerable. "You really hate me," he said blankly.

"Look at it my way. I live in the backwoods, and compared to you I'm destitute. Who would I hire to look after my interests? Mine and Daniel's. Sam Hailey from Deep Cove? Who comes here once a week to deal with parking tickets and the guys who think it's amusing to shoot holes in the town's two stop signs?"

"You must think I'm a real sleaze."

"You didn't make it to the top by being Mr. Nice."

"Let's try and get this discussion back on track," he said evenly. "I'd never try and take Daniel from you—apart from anything else, I don't imagine he'd let me. But I want to be part of his life, Shaine. To try and make up for lost time."

"What do you know about parenting? He's not two—he's twelve. A difficult age at the best of times. How do you think he's going to react to an unknown father suddenly appearing on the scene?"

It wasn't the moment for Jake to remember how his own eyes and Daniel's had locked together for a few brief moments at the rink; or how profoundly uneasy that contact had left him. What *did* he know about parenting? Nothing. Not one thing. He'd steered as clear of babies as he had of commitment. His friends tended to be singles, or couples who were putting off parenthood until they'd made their first million; which was the way he'd liked it. No fuss, no muss.

"I can learn," he said, wishing he sounded more convincing.

"Daniel's doing just fine without you. He has no lack of male role models, my three brothers see to that. His marks are good, he loves hockey, he has lots of friends. He doesn't need a father appearing out of the blue."

She ran her fingers through her tangled curls, trying to ignore the conflict in Jake's face. "There's something else you haven't even thought of—this is Daniel's home. Cranberry Cove. Not New York City. You'll tear him apart if you make him spend weekends and holidays with you, and then dump him back here for the rest of the time. After a while, he won't know where his home is."

"People are more important than places."

"His people are here," she said stonily. "Go away and forget about us, Jake. You're good at that."

"It's too late—I can't just forget that I have a son," Jake said savagely.

In a gesture that shocked him with its violence, she kicked the nearest rock with her foot. "You're like this granite—immovable!"

He gave an unexpected laugh. "You're like a she-wolf fighting for her cub."

"And why wouldn't I be?"

"You're also exactly like me—stubborn's your middle name."

"We've got to stop this," she cried. "Daniel's far too important for us to be standing here trading insults."

"Finally there's something we can agree on."

Jake wasn't going to go away, Shaine realized with a sick feeling in her belly; nothing she'd said had made any impression on him. But there was one more tack she hadn't tried. She said levelly, "I want you to do me a favor."

"Depends what it is."

"I want you to leave the cove this morning without seeing Daniel. I want you to go back to New York and think very hard about whether you really do want to be a father. Because if there's something I've learned in the last twelve years, it's that parenting is one of the biggest commitments there is. I'd be willing to bet you're commitment-phobic."

"Until now, I have been—and you're partly responsible for that," he said in a steel voice. "But I didn't just have to be ruthless to get to the top—I had to be flexible. Willing to change. Open to new possibilities."

"Daniel's not a business deal!"

"Don't insult me more than you already have."

She had the grace to look momentarily ashamed of herself. "I'm sorry," she muttered. "But I haven't finished. I want you to take a whole week and think about this. At the end of the week, you can phone me. I'll give you the telephone number of the shop, so you don't talk to Daniel by mistake."

Her voice suddenly shaky, she stretched out one hand in unconscious supplication. "Don't you see, Jake? This is a decision that can change three lives irrevocably, in ways we can't possibly anticipate. And one of those three lives is Daniel's—he's only twelve years old. This is much too significant for you to make a rash decision that's based on anger."

Jake felt a sudden rush of respect for the woman who'd just abandoned her pride to plead. He, better than most, knew how proud Shaine could be. And she was right. He was angry. Angry and hurt and, deep down, afraid. "If, after thinking about it, I say I want a part in Daniel's life, will you fight me on that, Shaine?"

"No," she said quietly, "I won't."

There was a lump in his throat. Swallowing hard, he said, "You've learned a lot by staying in the cove."

"I wouldn't have expected you to understand that."

She looked exhausted. Jake took two steps forward and enfolded her in his arms. She fit perfectly, just as she had so long ago. In a gesture that touched him to the core, she rested her forehead on his shoulder. "So you'll do it?" she whispered.

"Yes."

She sagged in his embrace. It wasn't lust he was feeling, at least not predominantly, Jake realized. It was tenderness. Not sure he wanted to pursue that thought, he said, "I won't call you on the weekend because of Daniel. How about a week from Monday around ten in the morning?"

"Fine."

Something in her voice alerted him. He raised her chin with one hand, seeing a bright shimmer of tears clinging to her lashes. "Shaine, don't," he said helplessly, "I never could stand it when you cried."

The faintest of smiles curved her lips. "Remember when I failed algebra?"

"All I had in my pocket was a handkerchief I'd used to wipe my skate blades...yeah, I remember."

She grimaced. "And then you tutored me for six months—you were the toughest teacher I ever had."

"But you made 98 in the final exam." He grinned down at her. "Tell me what's the matter now."

Evading his gaze, she muttered, "Nothing."

"You've been lonely, haven't you?" he said with the air of a man who's just had a blinding insight.

"Oh, shush. This is about Daniel, not about me."

"Not sure how to separate the two of you. If you let me into his life, I can help out. Financially, of course, that goes without saying. But—"

"You can't buy him!" she said, panic-stricken. Wasn't

that another of her many fears? How could Daniel be immune to the kind of money Jake had? No young boy would be.

"Just when I start to think we're acting like reasonable human beings, you belt me one," Jake rasped. "If I'm that bad, why aren't you setting the local police chief on me?"

"Jake, I've got to go—Daniel'll be home from hockey in the next few minutes and we can't risk him meeting you. Will you go back to the road through the woods?"

He nodded reluctantly. "I'm parked outside your shop."

She stepped away from him, gazing out at the ocean as though she'd never seen it before. "Goodbye," she said.

He didn't like the finality in her tone. Not one bit. Because it reminded him of how she'd said goodbye to him all those years ago, her lips set stubbornly in just the same way?

He was older now, and he'd learned a thing or two. He said equably, "Goodbye, Shaine. In case I decide I don't want to meet Daniel, I should tell you I'll be making a monthly deposit in a savings account for him in a bank in Corner Brook—I'll let you know the details. That way, he'll have more options for whatever he decides to do with his life."

"You can't do that!"

"Try and stop me," he said.

"I won't touch the money."

"That's right, you won't—it'll be in his name."

She looked as though she was about to explode. Giving her a bland smile, Jake walked away from her. He hadn't imagined that flash of disappointment in her eyes, he knew he hadn't: Shaine had been expecting—hoping?—he'd kiss her goodbye.

He'd wanted to, of course he had. But she didn't have to know that.

Shaine stayed where she was as Jake's back retreated through the trees. Now that he knew about Daniel, her terror should have abated. But it hadn't. If anything, it was worse.

She tried very hard to think calmly and logically. If Jake decided he didn't want to meet their son, she didn't have to worry.

But what if that wasn't his decision? What then?

Was she afraid of losing Daniel?

She sat down on the rocks, watching a flock of eiders wheel over the waves. Jake was forceful, ruthless and charismatic; she, of all people, knew that. He was also extraordinarily rich. If Jake decided he wanted Daniel, how could she withstand him?

I'd never try and take Daniel from you. But could she believe him? Years ago he'd destroyed her ability to trust. She'd believed in the bedrock of their friendship just as she believed in the hardness of the granite on which she was sitting. But Jake, in those long years of silence after he'd left the cove, had betrayed friendship in a way she'd been too young and too idealistic to anticipate.

Betrayal: a powerful and frightening word.

Shaine clasped her hands tightly in her lap and prayed with all her strength that she'd never see Jake again.

CHAPTER FOUR

Two days later, when Jake stepped from the cabin cruiser onto the wharf of the seaside resort, his first thought was that Shaine would like it here; his second that Daniel probably would, too, despite the boy's love of ice hockey.

Who could not like it?

He was on one of the forest-clad islands lodged between the mountainous shoreline and the Great Barrier Reef in Queensland. The island's own reef encircled it with clear turquoise water, and was encircled in turn by water of a much deeper blue. Blue like his son's eyes, Jake had thought as his plane had come in to land. Was it coincidence that he was about as far from Cranberry Cove as it was possible to get? "Hello, Ma," he said, and embraced his petite, determinedly brunette mother with genuine affection.

"I'm so glad you came to join us for a few days," Anna Sarton said. "This vacation is one of the nicest birthday presents I've ever had, thank you so much, Jake." She smiled fondly at her second husband. "Except for Henry, of course. We met on my birthday, did I ever tell you that, darling?"

Jake grinned. "Several times. Ma, you look great." Then he gave his stepfather a hug. "Good to see you, Henry."

"You must be ready for a swim," his mother said. "The ocean pools are wonderful, and they bring your drinks and snacks right to the edge of the water."

His mother had never quite been able to shake off her upbringing in a small and often harsh Newfoundland fishing village; her sense of wonder at all the world had to offer was one of her many likable traits. She and Henry

51

refused to accept any regular support from Jake; so he made sure they had at least three luxury-laden holidays a year. "A swim would be great," he said. "Get the kinks out."

The next few days should have been guaranteed to get any number of kinks out; especially when Jake was working so hard at having a good time. He knew he couldn't sit down and rationally decide what he was going to do about Shaine and Daniel; he had to wait until the answer became clear to him. In the meantime, he intended to play and play hard. He snorkeled, went scuba diving, kayaking, and sailing. He danced in the clubs at night, not always with his mother. He flirted.

None of it worked. The women, scantily clad and sending out signals galore that they were available, were not Shaine. The young boys vacationing with their parents reminded him painfully of Daniel. Six of the nine days before he was to phone Shaine with his decision fled past.

Who was occupying more of his thoughts, his son or Shaine? If she'd appeared at poolside in a bikini made of fake emeralds on tiny scraps of fabric, like the blonde who was sending suggestive glances his way, he'd have thrown her over his shoulder, taken her to his flower-bedecked bedroom and made love to her until neither one of them could walk across the room, let alone back to the pool.

He didn't want the blonde, gorgeous though she was. He wanted argumentative, fiery-haired Shaine, too thin, obstinate as the cliffs of the cove and twice as dangerous.

If he took an active role in his son's life, he'd be in contact with Shaine for at least the next six years.

If he took an active role? What choice did he have? Hadn't the decision been made in the rink when he and his son had stared at each other for what had felt like ten minutes and had probably been no more than ten seconds? He couldn't walk away from Daniel. He'd never be able to live with himself if he did that.

Blood really was thicker than water, Jake thought moodily, watching the salt drops dry on his bare thighs. He'd like to teach Daniel scuba diving. But he didn't even know if the boy knew how to swim...

"What's wrong, darling?" Anna said, briefly resting her bejeweled fingers on his arm. "You don't seem yourself."

They were sitting in the shade of the awnings. Henry had gone for a swim, and most of the other holiday makers were eating lunch. Jake glanced over at his mother. Not the least of his dilemmas was whether he had the right to keep from her that she had a grandson.

He said in a clipped voice, "I went back to Cranberry Cove last week. First time since you moved to Australia."

She shivered, her face looking suddenly pinched. "I've never gone back. I couldn't bear to after your father drowned. And, as you know, my best friend Bertha had moved away a few months before that. So there really was nothing to take me back. I didn't even keep in touch with people. Not very admirable of me, I suppose, but that's the way it was."

"I saw Shaine."

"She's still there? That surprises me."

"It surprised me, too," Jake said wryly.

"I always liked Shaine...I was glad when you befriended her."

"I fell in love with her, Ma—right after Dad died."

"I wondered if that's what had happened...I wasn't a good mother to you in those last few weeks at the cove."

"You did the best you could," Jake said gruffly. "Shaine stayed behind when I left, even though she'd promised to leave with me." He took a gulp of his cold beer. "Near to broke my heart."

"You never told me that."

"Never told anyone. Except Shaine, last week." He paused, gazing into the bubbles rising inexorably to the surface, and knew he couldn't stop there. "There's more. Shaine and I made love, just once, the day I left. Last week

I found out that I have a son. His name's Daniel, he's twelve.''

"Shaine has a son?"

"Your grandson, Ma."

Anna sat bolt upright. "Grandson?" she squeaked.

"Yeah...I don't blame you for being angry, I should've gotten in touch with Shaine years—"

"Angry?" Anna interrupted. "Who says I'm angry?"

He looked over at her. A beatific smile had spread over her plump, pretty face, and her eyes, blue as his own, were sparkling. "But he's twelve," Jake said, "you've missed so much."

"Then I'll make up for lost time," Anna said ebulliently. "I've longed for grandchildren, Jake, and you've shown no signs of settling down. Now I have a ready-made one. When do I get to meet him?"

"I've never met him. That's why I came here. To figure out what I was going to do."

Shocked, Anna said, "But you'll go back. You're his father."

"Yes, I'll go back. I want him to spend some time with me in the Hamptons and Manhattan...I'll invite you and Henry when he's there."

"Aren't you going to marry Shaine?"

He winced. "Wasn't planning on it."

"But you're still in love with her." His mother added vigorously, "You must be in love if you could ignore that blonde—she was just about falling out of her bra."

"So you noticed."

"Difficult not to," Anna snorted. "Are you in love with Shaine?"

"No! Well...no."

Anna hid a small smile. "When are you going back to the cove?"

"I have a day's business in Thailand. Then I'll fly to Vancouver and head east."

"Do you have a photo of Daniel?"

"Not yet, no." Warming to his subject in a way that was very telling, Jake described all that he knew about the boy. "Shaine likely spends as much time at the rink as you did, Ma."

"She'd be a good mother...you could do a lot worse than marrying Shaine."

"Tell her that," he said lightly.

"That's your job," Anna said. "May I share this with Henry?"

"Sure...and thanks for listening."

"Thanks for telling me." Anna patted his hand and got up to join Henry in the water. "You'll do what's right, Jake."

Did that mean marrying Shaine? Surely not. Besides, a hundred to one she'd say no. Jake got up, too, stretched, and went in search of lunch.

But not in search of the blonde.

Cranberry Cove was wreathed in fog when Jake made the slow descent down Breakheart Hill. He'd phoned Shaine, as promised, last Monday from Thailand, telling her he wanted to be a part of his son's life but hadn't yet figured out how he was going to go about that. "I don't want you telling him about me," he'd finished. "Not yet."

"Don't you trust me?" she'd responded edgily.

It was a good question. "There's not much point in me making all kinds of plans for the future if he's not interested," Jake answered evasively. "As you so rightly pointed out, he's not two, he's twelve. With a mind of his own. Maybe I want to meet him at the rink, where we have something in common."

"I think I should warn him."

"I'm not going to abduct him—give me a break, Shaine."

"I'm used to making all the decisions myself!"

"One thing about you," he said dryly, "I can always count on you to tell it like it is. I want to add something to Daniel's life, for Pete's sake, not harm him. Don't *you* trust *me?*"

A very expensive pause hummed over the line. "How can I possibly answer that?" she said irritably.

"Think about it. I'll be in touch," he said, and slammed down the phone before she could reply.

Shaine, so far, didn't know he was coming today. Which didn't mean he distrusted her. Rather, he didn't want her running interference for him, setting up the first, fraught meeting between father and son. There was no easy way to tell Daniel that the man who'd fathered him and then vanished was now back in the picture. It was up to him, Jake, to do that. He was the one who'd left and hadn't kept in touch with the boy's mother. It was his job to make reparation, not Shaine's.

All of which had sounded fine as he'd sat in his private jet winging across the country from Vancouver to Deer Lake. Now, when the first houses were emerging from the mist, Jake wasn't so sure. He pulled over and rested his forearms on the wheel. He was as scared of a twelve-year-old boy as he'd been of the president of that first corporation he'd approached. Hell, who was he fooling? He'd never felt like this in his whole life.

If only he hadn't had that dream. He'd spent the night in Toronto at a hotel airport, trying to absorb some jet lag before flying further east. He'd dreamed about Shaine on Ghost Island in her blue dress...or had it been a dream? Had it, simply, been memory rising from his subconscious before he was fully awake?

He and Shaine had moored the dory to the old jetty, using a rusty ring sunk into the wood. Then they'd climbed to the meadow on the far side of the island, where the automatic lighthouse stood sentinel by the reef, and wildflowers raised petals like colored stars in the grass. It was there that they'd seen the humpback whales.

Shaine said, "I brought a picnic."

Her blue dress had a flared skirt that dipped to mid-calf, and could by no means be called overtly sexy. But everything she wore was sexy to Jake. He was obsessed with her, day and night; and had never laid as much as a finger on her for just that reason. She'd only turned eighteen the month before, whereas he was twenty-two. He'd lived for over four years away from the confines of the cove; it was up to him to keep her safe.

"Chicken sandwiches?" he said hopefully. He'd been working in the woods since he'd come back for his father's funeral, hard physical labor that left him with a prodigious appetite.

"Of course. They're your favorite, aren't they?"

She seemed edgy, he thought, not her usual self, although he had no idea why. He spread the blanket on the grass, sitting on one corner as far from her as he could get, and started to eat. She said, "I don't have a communicable disease, Jake."

He raised one brow. "This way I can look at you."

"That's all you ever do!"

His hand stilled. "What do you mean?"

She put down her sandwich, uneaten, and ripped the ribbon from her hair so that it blew free in the wind like a curtain of fire. "I want you to make love to me."

"*What?*"

"Here. Today."

Her eyes were defiant rather than loving. Faint blue shadows were pooled below her collarbones, while her lips were soft pink curves, so voluptuous he had to look away. "I'm leaving here in a couple of days," he said. "You know that. You're coming with me. Don't you think we should wait until we're more sure of—"

"No, I don't." She leaned forward, her breasts moving

suggestively under the thin cotton of her dress. "We love each other. Why wait? Why not seize what the day has to offer?"

"I don't have any protection," he said.

"I'm in the safest part of my cycle, we'll be all right." She tossed her head. "Unless you don't want to make love with me."

"I want to make love to you so badly I can't sleep at night," he said roughly. "Every day in the woods all I can think about is you. I love you, Shaine, I'll love you forever."

She smiled, the smile of a woman who knew exactly what she wanted. "Come here," she said softly.

Take it easy, he told himself. This is her first time, you've got to make it perfect for her. But when he found her mouth with his, he groaned deep in his throat, so heated was her response, so recklessly alive and openly hungry. "I don't want to rush you," he muttered.

"I want you," she whispered, nipping his bottom lip with her teeth, her nails digging into his shoulders. Then he felt the first dart of her tongue, and lost all his good resolutions as heat throbbed through his veins. Shaine had never been someone to do things by half measures; and now was no exception. Her own ardor, touchingly inexperienced, inflamed his senses. He kissed her deeply, savoring the sweetness of her mouth, aware through every nerve of the softness of her breasts against his chest, of the instinctive and infinitely seductive movements of her hips beneath his.

He found the swell of one breast, cupping it, playing with the nipple through her dress; then, fiercely impatient, he unbuttoned the bodice. Her bra was blue, too. She said with endearing shyness, because Shaine was rarely shy, "I ordered it through the catalog. Just for you."

"I've been staying away from you for weeks because I

was afraid this would happen. You don't know how often I've wanted to kiss you, touch you, hold on to you.''

She gave an exultant laugh, slipping her fingers under his T-shirt to caress the rough, dark hair that funneled to his navel. "There's nothing to be afraid of." Her irises darkened as he played with her nipple, her breath coming in small gasps of pleasure. "I want to be naked," she whispered. "I want to feel you all the way down my body."

He sat up, hauling his shirt over his head and tossing it to one side. Then, more gently, he tugged her dress upward so that momentarily the vivid brightness of her hair was eclipsed. Swiftly he unclasped her bra, then slid her blue panties down her hips. For a moment that was outside of time, all he could do was gaze at her, all his love and longing exposed for her to read. She said huskily, "Jake, Jake...when you look at me like that, I melt inside."

He ran his hand from her shoulder to her flank, as though memorizing every curve. "You're so beautiful...your skin's white as foam."

"Your eyes are like the sea," she said, and reached for his belt. Within moments his clothes were tossed aside and his bare thighs had pinned her to the blanket, his big body hovering over her before, once more, he plunged for the honey of her mouth. His hands roamed her body, her fevered moans of hunger ravishing his senses.

She smelled sweetly of flowers, she even tasted of flowers, while her skin was smooth as rose petals. She was his heart's desire, his only love...and open to him as the rose opens to the sun. He found the gap between her thighs, where she was moist and ready, and rhythmically rubbed all his hardness against her until she was panting and writhing. Then she cried his name, once, twice, and he felt the inner throbbing as she climaxed.

Briefly she collapsed beneath him. "I couldn't wait," she gasped. "But, Jake—"

"Hush," he said, and subduing his own needs, began

laving her nipple with his tongue. Then he moved lower, stroking the dip of her belly and the tautness of rib, cupping her buttocks and lifting her to meet his hungry tongue. She threw back her head, enraptured, and within moments her small, broken sobs of fulfillment filled his ears again, like the most elemental music in the world.

But he wasn't done with her. Rolling over, so that she lay across him, he said, "Straddle me, Shaine. Touch me."

Her eyes glittering a pagan green, she reared up, sun and shadow playing with her breasts. Exquisitely shaped breasts, Jake thought, his mouth dry. He couldn't last much longer. But greater than his own passionate ache to be inside her, was the sheer heaven of watching her discover her own sensuality. She said, smiling down at him, "Now it's my turn."

"I love you, Shaine," he said harshly.

She bent forward, her rippled hair drifting over his chest and face, scented and silky. Her breasts brushed his nipples with hypnotic smoothness until he wondered if he could die from sheer pleasure. And all the while her hands were exploring his body, her palms fitting to the hard arc of his shoulders, her fingers playing with his body hair. Then, very gently, she lowered herself onto him, her warmth encompassing him until he could scarcely breathe. He watched the fleeting expressions on her face, each one so precious to him. She was wet and open; but even so there was that moment of resistance, a flash of pain crossing her features.

As carefully as he could, he pushed into her. Then, suddenly, her whole weight was resting on him. Wonderment suffusing her face, she leaned forward to kiss him. He thrust, harder and harder, seeing the storm gather in her eyes even as his own inner tumult became almost unbearable.

They broke at the same time, their hoarse cries entangled like the screams of gulls against the heavens. Then she was lying on top of him, her heart hammering against his ribs, his own heart pounding like surf on the beach...

A transport truck emerged through the fog, startling Jake from his reverie. So who *was* he coming back to see? His son, Daniel? Or Shaine? Who, when he'd mentioned only minutes after that passionate lovemaking that they'd be leaving the cove and Newfoundland in the next two days, had told him that she couldn't leave. That she'd changed her mind.

At first she wouldn't tell him why. But when he'd persisted, she'd destroyed all his hopes, all his faith in her, by saying she didn't love him enough to go away with him.

Devastated, he'd left without her that very day.

He'd been licking his wounds ever since. His affairs had been enjoyable enough, but bloodless. He hadn't even come close to falling in love. And all because of a red-haired woman whose heart had captured his, and whose body had bewitched him.

Whose body had borne him a son.

He'd come back here to meet Daniel. That was all.

Slowly Jake drove the narrow streets of the village. It was late afternoon, the light opaque and mysterious. He passed the turnoff to Shaine's house and didn't stop. He should at least have formulated a plan, he thought caustically. Hadn't he, for the last thirteen years, lived by nothing but plans?

And then his heart thudded in his chest. A young boy was walking along the sidewalk, a hockey bag slung across one shoulder. Jake would have recognized him anywhere.

Knowing that his action was momentous, he drew up level with the boy. "Going to the rink? Want a drive?"

Daniel's blue eyes widened; for a moment he stood stock-still. Then he said, in a voice deeper than Jake had expected, "Sure, thanks."

He climbed in on the passenger side after tossing his gear

in the back seat. "I saw you at the rink ten days ago," he said.

Jake hadn't expected such a direct approach. "That's right. I'm Jake Reilly. I used to live here."

"Yeah, I know."

"You *do?*"

"Down at the high school, they've got pictures from the year your team won the trophy. That day at the rink I recognized you right away."

"Oh," said Jake with a notable lack of intelligence.

"Why'd you come back?"

"I left the village for good thirteen years ago," Jake said carefully. "I figured it was time I saw the place where I was born." He turned into the rink and parked an equally careful distance from the door.

"No, I mean why'd you come back here today—for the second time?"

"I—I had some unfinished business."

"After I saw your picture at the school, I looked you up on the Internet," Daniel said with an edge of aggressiveness.

His jaw tight with tension, Jake asked, "Why did you do that?"

The boy shrugged. "Dunno. I just did. Found out you went away to university and came home when your father died. Then my mum had this financial magazine, and you were in that, too. They had a lot of pictures of you in places like Singapore, and then dancing with a woman they said was your companion in a club in New York."

Her name had been Marilee, Jake recalled. Although he was damned if he could remember one more thing about her. "I left the cove because I needed wider horizons," he said.

"There's nothing wrong with Cranberry Cove!"

"No, there isn't. I didn't fit here, that's all."

"I played hockey in Maine last year—but I was glad to

get home," Daniel said defiantly. "Where d'you play now?"

"I don't."

"You don't?"

The boy looked as horrified as if Jake had confessed to murder. "I've been too busy," Jake said. "But ever since watching you play, I've been thinking I should get back to it."

"Someone told me you and Mum used to be friends."

"That's right," Jake said steadily. "She's a fine woman, your mother. Daniel, I need to talk to you about something. Can we meet after your game?"

The boy tensed. "What's wrong with now? I'm early. Figured I'd practice shots on goal while I was waiting."

It was now or never, Jake thought fatalistically, looking straight into the blue eyes that were so like his own; although they were, right now, clouded with apprehension. "I came back the second time because there's something I have to tell you," he said. "Thirteen years ago your mother and I were, very briefly, lovers. When I came back here a couple of weeks ago, I found out that she'd had a son a few months after I left." He paused, his heartbeat crowding into his throat. "You're my son, Daniel."

The boy let out his breath in a small whoosh. "Ever since I saw your picture at the school, I kinda wondered," he said. "Seeing as how O'Sullivans don't have dark hair or blue eyes."

"How long ago did you see the picture?" Jake demanded.

"Three or four years."

"So that's why you looked me up on the Internet?"

"Guess so." Daniel was gazing out into the fog. He'd outgrown his jacket; his wrists stuck out of the sleeves, Jake noticed with the only part of his brain that seemed to be working. It touched him unbearably. Wanting to enfold the boy in his arms, he sat still and waited.

Daniel said hoarsely, "How come it took you thirteen years to come and see me?"

"I didn't know you existed until ten days ago!"

"If you were friends with my mum, why didn't you keep in touch with her?"

It was the most difficult question Daniel could have asked. Yet he deserved a truthful answer. "I was in love with your mother. But she wouldn't come away with me even though we'd planned that. So I left and didn't look back. My father had drowned here, my mother had emigrated to Australia, I had no ties with the place."

"You were too busy making money and dating other women," Daniel said in a hostile voice.

"The first part of that statement's true enough. The second isn't. I haven't married, or wanted to."

"Mum never got a cent of your money. Or a moment of your time. She had to do it all on her own."

Refusing to back down, Jake said, "That's right. I regret more than I can say that I didn't get in touch with her. That I've missed all these years of knowing you."

"I haven't missed you. I've done just fine without you."

Daniel was, unconsciously, paraphrasing what his mother had said. "Yes, you have," Jake said. He allowed a smile to break through. "I hate to admit it, but I reckon that in a couple of years you'll be a better hockey player than I was."

Daniel's lashes, long as a girl's, dropped to hide his eyes. He was going to be a handsome young man, Jake thought. Put that together with his hockey skills, and the girls would be after him in droves. "Daniel," he said urgently, "I just want to hang around with you a bit. Get to know you."

With something of his mother's quicksilver intelligence, Daniel pounced. "Hang around a bit," he repeated cynically. "That says it all. Hang around as long as it suits you, then go back to your real life."

"I want you to be part of my real life."

"What about my mum? What about her?"

"She's as angry as you are that I didn't keep in touch."

"You going to marry her?"

It was his own mother's question. "I don't think she'd marry me if her life depended on it," Jake said truthfully.

With deliberate crudity Daniel said, "You don't care that I get called names at school?"

Jake flinched. "Does that happen often?"

"It used to. Until Uncle Padric taught me how to fight."

Padric. Not the boy's father. With a sick lump in his gut, Jake said, "I'm sorry, Daniel. I'm really sorry I stayed away for so long."

The boy gave a dismissive shrug. "You got more important things to do than stick around here—you're a big shot." He reached for the door handle. "I don't need you any more than my mum does. Why should I?"

Jake took the boy by the sleeve. "I'm not going to go away like I did thirteen years ago. Not twice. So you'd better get used to seeing me around."

Daniel shook free and scrambled out of the car. "I'm gonna be late," he mumbled, grabbed his bag from the back seat and slammed both doors so loudly they sounded like twin gunshots. Then he ran for the door of the rink.

Jake knew better than to follow. He sat still, his emotions in a turmoil. If he'd cherished any fantasies of his son falling into his arms, he'd better abandon them fast. Daniel was as antagonistic toward him as Shaine.

With as much reason?

Regret, so Jake was discovering, was much harder to deal with than grief. He'd felt huge grief when his father had died, drowned by the sea that had sustained him most of his life. But that sadness had been natural, and in time had eased, leaving Jake with many good memories of the big, gentle man who'd loved him from the day he was born. But regret? What could he do about that? He couldn't undo the past and rewrite it the way he now wanted it to be. The past was just that: past. Both Shaine and Daniel had suffered because he himself had allowed pride, hurt and ambition to barricade him from the village where he'd grown up.

Daniel had never known the deep security of a father's love as he, Jake, had; the boy had been robbed of something that should be every child's heritage.

Jake's brow knit. Had it all been his fault? Or did Shaine bear some of the responsibility?

Years ago, he'd nearly driven himself crazy wondering why Shaine hadn't loved him enough to go away with him. Now, after a stormy reunion with her and a painful meeting with his son, he found himself chewing once again on that old bone. She wasn't someone to change her mind easily; and whatever she felt, she felt wholeheartedly. Had something happened to make her alter her plans so drastically?

Maybe it was time he found out. Demanded some answers of her. Because, of course, he was going to see her. There'd be no better opportunity than now, with Daniel safely at the rink for the next hour and a half.

What if Daniel really didn't want anything to do with him? What then?

Won't go there, Jake thought savagely, and backed out of the parking lot. The fog had thickened while he'd been talking to his son. Had he totally messed up his life? All his money wasn't much good to him if the woman he'd loved and the son she'd given birth to didn't want to spend the time of day with him.

Won't go there, either.

CHAPTER FIVE

JAKE parked near the craft shop. Lights gleamed through the tall windows. The stained-glass panel of the whales was, if anything, more striking than he'd remembered. He was going to buy it, he thought, pushing through the door. And if Shaine objected, too bad.

To his great relief, there were no customers in the shop. When Shaine looked up and saw him, she didn't faint. Progress, he thought, taking a moment to admire her slim curves in her bright orange tunic with its matching brief skirt.

"Hello," she said coolly. "Nice of you to let me know you were coming."

All his skills in diplomacy deserting him, he said, "I just gave Daniel a drive to the rink."

"You *what?*"

"He was walking along the sidewalk, so I stopped and picked him up."

In a wave of fury, Shaine planted her hands on her hips. "You were supposed to wait and talk to me before you spoke to him."

"Well, I didn't. And it makes no difference, anyway. Ever since he saw my photo in the hockey archives at the high school three or four years ago, he's suspected that I was his father."

She could feel the color draining from her face. "Is that what he said?"

"The kid's not stupid, Shaine. He could see that he and I have the same color hair and eyes. And when he put it together with my dad's funeral, the timing was right."

"He never told me!"

"He did an Internet search on me, and read those financial magazines you had. If it makes you any happier, he wasn't what you'd call delighted to meet me."

"So for months he's known the name of his father?" Stunned, feeling as though the world had shifted beneath her feet, she said, "I can't believe he wouldn't have asked me about you. Didn't he trust me?"

Jake rested a hand lightly on her bare arm. "He's only twelve—it's a loaded topic."

She stared down at Jake's hand as if it were an adder about to bite her. "He's angry with you?"

"You could say so." Restlessly Jake moved away, prowling around the shop like a trapped mountain lion. "Why wouldn't he be? Whether or not he said anything to you about his suspicions, don't ever doubt he loves you. One reason he's so angry with me is that you were left alone to bring him up, and with very little money—no support from me, in other words. While I, according to him, was stashing away millions, living like a king and having affairs with every woman in sight."

"Sounds accurate to me."

"Come off it," Jake said impatiently. "You should know me better than that."

The bell over the door tinkled as three customers walked in. The first of them, Jake saw with something akin to horror, was Maggie Stearns. Her pale blue eyes fastened on Jake like limpets to a rock. "Well, if it isn't Jake Reilly," she said genially, coming over and kissing him with damp enthusiasm on the cheek. "Someone told me you'd been in town. And now you're back. What brings you to these parts?"

"I've stayed away too long," Jake said with more regard for the truth than Maggie deserved.

"Thirteen years. I was saying to Shaine just the other day that I wished you'd dropped in for tea when you were here. How about this evening? Marty'd be real happy to see you.''

Her husband Marty, unless things had changed, busied himself making ships in bottles and rarely said a word. Out of the corner of his eye, Jake saw Shaine waiting with malicious pleasure for his reply. "Some other time, Maggie," he said. "Shaine's invited me for dinner this evening.''

A pink patch adorning each cheek, Shaine began, "That's not—''

"I was on my way to pick up a bottle of wine," Jake said, smiling at Maggie, "and thought I should check with Shaine whether she wanted white or red."

The other two customers were strangers to him. Tourists, he thought, and watched with amusement as Shaine struggled against the urge to tell him exactly where to go.

"I'm always partial to a glass of wine," Maggie said. "What are you cooking, Shaine?''

Brimstone and ashes, said Shaine's eyes. "Haddock," she said in a stifled voice.

"Then you'll want a nice dry Bordeaux. Just you ask Sammie at the liquor store, Jake, he'll help you pick one out. Why," she trilled, "I might have to drop in after supper myself and have a little glass. To welcome you home. How long are you staying this time?''

Mentally, Jake counted to ten. He was considered something of a connoisseur of wines; the last person he wanted to see tonight was Maggie; and he had no idea how long he was going to stay. He said cheerfully, "I'll see you some other time, Maggie—I'll be around long enough for that." He eyed the shopping bag in her hand. "So you're on your way home? Take care, won't you, and say hello to Marty for me."

Short of rudeness, Maggie had no choice but to leave the shop. As she flounced outside, Jake winked at Shaine. Unwilling respect and fury battling in her breast, she said sweetly, "If I'd remembered you were coming for supper tonight, I'd have made bakeapple pie."

Three summers in a row he and Shaine had picked bake-apples on the barrens along the coast and sold them to the local grocery store; the orange berries, shaped like black-berries but growing low to the ground, were much prized in the village. That was in the days when they'd been friends, he remembered, two adolescents who, despite the difference in age and gender, had found pleasure in each other's company. One point for you, he thought, and said, "I want to buy the whale panel, Shaine. Can you pack it up and ship it to Long Island?"

Whatever she might have expected him to say next, it wouldn't have been that. "You don't really want it—it's too expensive."

He tossed his platinum credit card on the counter. "Include the price of shipping, won't you?"

"What will you do with it?"

"Hang it in the window that overlooks the patio, watch the light move across it, and think of you."

"You must be hard up for kicks."

"Yeah," he said, "I'm beginning to think you're right... I'll be back shortly with the wine."

"You'd better buy two bottles—I'm going to invite all three of my brothers."

He laughed. "Tell them to leave their shotguns at home."

"It's too late for that, Jake."

"You always were a worthy opponent," he said affably, and marched out of the shop into the fog.

When had he felt as fully alive as he did now, walking down a narrow road, the sound of waves muffled by the mist, the air redolent with salt and seaweed? He was on his way to buy wine for a dinner that was almost guaranteed to be a social disaster. His son resented him, Shaine's three brothers no doubt felt the same way, and Shaine both desired him and hated the ground he walked on. Maybe he should buy a whole case of wine.

He settled for two bottles of a fairly decent Chilean Chardonnay. Then he continued down the street to Mrs. Emily Bennett's house. She opened the door herself, a plump widow in her sixties whose strong morals were sometimes in conflict with her kind heart. "Jake!" she exclaimed. "I heard you'd been in the village...come on in."

Stepping inside, he hugged her. "While I'm back, I'll come for a proper visit. But right now I'm hoping you can do me a favor. You wouldn't happen to have a bakeapple pie in your freezer, would you?"

"I made half a dozen the other day."

"I'm having supper at Shaine's, and I'd like to take her one."

"You're having supper at Shaine's?"

Her face was an open book. In a resigned voice Jake said, "So you've figured out that Daniel's my son?"

"Years ago. But I've never said a word to anyone."

"I didn't know about him, Emily. Not until two weeks ago."

"That's because you left this place fast as a wild pony leaves the corral."

How could he deny it? "Daniel doesn't want anything to do with me."

"He'll come 'round. What about Shaine?"

"Same."

"Well...I'll go get the pie. A bakeapple pie can do wonders."

Melt Shaine's obdurate heart? Jake didn't think so.

A few minutes later Emily came upstairs from the basement, puffing a little. "How long are you staying?"

"Don't know yet."

"Are you planning to make an honest woman out of Shaine?"

"Shaine's as honest a woman as you are, Emily, and that's got nothing to do with her marital status."

"It's about time that boy had a father. Three uncles are no substitute for the real thing."

"Shaine wouldn't marry me if she'd had quintuplets," he said in exasperation.

"Then you'd better stick around long enough to change her mind." Emily handed him the pie, her smile breaking through. "Fine-looking man like you, you'll have no trouble putting a ring on Shaine's finger...don't you forget to come for a visit, now."

"I'll be by in the next couple of days," he promised, and started back the way he'd come. Did the entire village know he was Daniel's father? Was the boy being taunted at school and at the rink about Jake's return? Along with Shaine's lack of a wedding ring?

Finding he could scarcely stand his own thoughts, Jake saw the yellow house loom through the fog. Impulsively he took a detour through the tall wet grass toward the cliffs. When he found what he was looking for, he put the pie down on top of the bottles of wine, and bent to his task. Then he walked back toward the house.

The lights were on inside. Blurred by the fog, Shaine was standing at the sink, wearing trim-fitting jeans and a fuchsia sweater that clashed with her hair. If only he could walk in the door and take her to bed. If only life were that simple.

She'd go. He was willing to bet she would. Wild images of her naked in his arms flitted through Jake's head, setting his pulses racing. He'd never, technically, been to bed with Shaine; they'd made love on the island on a blanket spread on the grass.

Was sex the way to bring her around, or was he better to work on the wholly platonic friendship they'd shared for so many years? Wasn't it near here that he'd first come across her? He'd been jogging the cliff path, his CD player clipped to his waist...

Jake circled the rocks, oblivious to anything but the music in his ears and the rhythm of his feet on the grass. A girl was crouched in the shadow of the rocks. He swerved, flinging out a hand so he wouldn't trip. She was crying, slow tears seeping down pale cheeks under a mop of tangled red curls.

Jake stopped dead, his chest heaving. At thirteen, he wasn't interested in girls who were years younger than he. Especially if they were crying. He yanked off his ear plugs and said reluctantly, "You okay?"

"I'm fine."

Her lips were a mutinous line, although her eyes shimmered like dew on the early morning grass. On the flat rock beside her was a sketch pad; as he looked at it, she scrambled to cover it with her hands. "Hold on," he said, interested, "let me see."

"Go away!"

He almost did. After all, whatever was bothering her had nothing to do with him. But then he stooped, pushing her hands aside and stared at the page. She'd created a pinwheel of colors in jagged fragments that captured to perfection the profusion of wildflowers that surrounded them. "It's beautiful," he said.

She scowled at him. "You're just saying that so I'll stop crying."

"Girls crying make me crazy." He grinned. "But I meant what I said. You must get top marks in art. I flunked it last term—you've got to work hard to flunk art."

"The teacher thinks I should stick to the class assignments and quit making all these weird designs."

"That's old man Mulligan for you. The guy's a jerk."

The first inkling of a smile tugged at her mouth. "I hate him," she said.

"Do his stupid assignments if that's what keeps him happy. But don't stop doing these. Just don't show 'em to him."

"You really do like it? Why?"

"I don't know," Jake said, nonplussed. "I flunked art, remember? I just like the way it swirls, that's all. Like when I'm on the rink—you can hear the wind."

Her cheeks flushed with pleasure. "The other kids think I'm weird, too. I didn't get invited to Sally Hatchet's birthday party. It's tonight."

"Is that why you were crying?"

"Sort of. But I can't stop being me!"

On impulse, Jake passed her his headset. "Listen for a minute."

She did so, her face puckered with attention. "I never heard music like that before."

"Classical. Baroque period. Albinoni's Concerto for Oboe. Guys aren't supposed to listen to stuff like that. I'm always getting into fights at school because I hate rap and I'm top of my class without having to study. Lucky for me I'm a hockey star, saves my bacon."

"So you don't fit in, either," she said slowly.

"Nope. It doesn't matter as much as I used to think it did. If that's any help."

"Girls don't have fist fights at school. They just shut you out of all the girl things they do."

"Tell you what, then. How about every so often you and I go for a walk? Or out in my dad's boat. Or berry picking. I'll listen to music and you can paint pictures and no one'll tell us we oughta like punk rock and sissy pictures of kittens."

She laughed outright, a delightful cascade of sound. "Okay," she said, "I'd like that. I'm Shaine O'Sullivan, I live in the yellow house by the cliffs."

"Jake Reilly. We live on Main Street." They shook hands solemnly. "I'll call you in a couple of days. My dad might be going out to Ghost Island on the weekend, the wild strawberries are ripe.''

That had been the beginning, Jake thought. A handshake, and then a sun-soaked day picking the berries that nestled in the low grass on the island. For years it had been an undemanding friendship, perhaps the deeper because of all they hadn't needed to say. When he went away to university at seventeen, they'd exchanged letters; he hadn't been home for nearly five years, because of hockey, his fanatic ambition to top his class, and two jobs every summer to pay for his tuition and board. Then he'd come back when his father had drowned, and found, instead of the young girl he'd remembered, a beautiful young woman. A stranger who wasn't a stranger, and all the more seductive because of it...that was when he'd fallen in love.

He gave his head a little shake. Mist had settled on his shirt, and the legs of his jeans were wet. Time to go indoors. Time to face the family, he thought ruefully, and squared his shoulders.

He was still nuts about baroque music, although it had taken an unorthodox mathematics professor to ally that with his genius for numbers. What kind of music did Daniel like?

Another huge blank.

He walked up the steps and knocked on the back door. Shaine opened it. He said, thrusting his offerings at her, "Two bottles of wine, a bakeapple pie and roses."

They were brier roses from the cliffs. As Shaine, conspicuously, said nothing, Jake labored on, "No flower shop in Cranberry Cove. As you know."

They were very simple gifts. No need for her to feel as though she'd been given the moon and the stars. When she thought she could trust her voice, she said, "Where did you get the pie?"

"I have my contacts."

"I wish you didn't make me laugh," Shaine said ferociously. "I wish I didn't like you when I can't stand the sight of you."

Astonishingly pleased by this incoherent speech, Jake said, "I shed good blood for those roses. Be careful when you put them in water, the thorns are vicious."

"Are they supposed to be a metaphor?"

"For what?" he said blandly. "You?"

"For life in general," she said, scowling at him. "Since you're already bleeding, why don't you put them in water while I thaw the pie? There's a vase in the cupboard over the sink."

He put the roses on the counter and advanced on her. "You're supposed to say thank you."

Frightened out of her wits, Shaine wielded a flour-coated wooden spoon at him. "Neither one of us was ever much good at doing what we were supposed to."

He grabbed the spoon with one hand and her waist with the other. But because at the last moment she turned her head, his kiss landed on her cheek rather than her mouth. Tightening his hold, Jake slid his lips with sensuous pleasure down the taut line of her jaw to her throat. "You smell nice," he murmured, "and you taste better. Too bad you've got three brothers and a son, or do you know where we'd be?"

"In this village? You're joking—Maggie'd know what we were up to before we did."

Her eyes had a jewel-like brilliance, while her body was as pliant as those long-ago wildflowers in the wind. Throwing caution out the door, Jake said, "Despite that glossy magazine, I haven't had very many women, Shaine. Too picky. But in thirteen years there's never been a woman like you. Never. I just have to look at you and—"

The back door slammed. Shaine pulled free and stuck the spoon into the wrong pot. "Put the roses in a vase, Jake."

So when Daniel came into the kitchen, Jake was standing at the sink filling a tall glass vase with water. "Hi, Daniel," he said.

Daniel's eyes flew to his mother. "What's he doing here?"

To Jake's enormous gratification, she said calmly, "I invited him for supper. It'll be twenty minutes, you've got time to shower."

"He's my father!"

"Yes, he is." Her heart racing against her ribs, she said, "I know this is difficult, Daniel. For both of us. But Jake's here and he wants to get to know you."

His feet planted on the worn linoleum, Daniel said, "I'll eat upstairs. I've got homework."

"Your uncles are coming and we're all eating in the dining room. Go have a shower."

Daniel was the exact same height as his mother; but it was his eyes that fell. He slouched out of the room and Jake heard him banging his way up the stairs. He said flatly, "It was more than generous of you to hide the fact that I invited myself for supper."

"I'm trying to do what's best for him. Not for you," she snapped. "What with him sassing me and you kissing me, it'll be a wonder if I ever get supper on the table."

Angry, yielding, passionate and stubborn...how could he not be drawn to her like the river to the sea? Not that this was the time or the place to pursue that particular thought. "What can I do to help?"

"Set six places at the dining room table and put the roses on the cabinet."

Jake did as he was told, and was mashing potatoes when Shaine's three brothers came in procession through the back door: Devlin, who had carrot-orange hair; Padric with his chestnut curls; and Connor, whose straight auburn hair was tied back with a piece of lobster twine. Not one of them looked the least bit welcoming. They looked, Jake thought, as though they would take considerable pleasure in tearing him limb from limb.

Let 'em try.

He greeted each of them in turn as casually as if he'd never moved away. Devlin plunked a jar of pickles on the table, Padric a six-pack of beer, and Connor, empty-handed, kissed his sister on the cheek. "Daniel back?" he asked, slanting a glance at Jake.

"He's showering," Shaine said.

"What does he think about all this?"

"He's not wild about it."

"That makes four of us," Padric drawled, bouncing gently on the balls of his feet as he uncapped a beer with his fingers.

"Don't stir up more trouble than we've got," Shaine ordered. "There's wine in the fridge, Connor. Pour me a glass, will you?"

Connor reached into the refrigerator and pulled out one of the bottles. He gave an exaggerated whistle. "High-class stuff. Guess who brought this."

Jake said softly, "The four of us can go out in the field after dinner and punch each other out if that's what you want. But for now let's try and behave like civilized human beings. For Daniel's sake, if for no other reason."

"He's right," Devlin said in his gravelly bass voice. "Settle down, you two."

Jake would never forget that interminable dinner. Daniel said nothing unless directly addressed, and then answered only in monosyllables. Shaine alternated between a tight-lipped silence and outbursts of babbling that were totally unlike her. The three brothers, by an unspoken pact, were crushingly polite. As for Jake, he heard himself being the suave city slicker, and couldn't seem to stop. He was the one who'd instigated this, he thought. He must have been clean crazy.

"Great fish," he said, trying to end a silence broken only

by Shaine clearing away the plates. "Better than anything you can get in New York."

"Took you long enough to come back for it," Connor said with deceptive mildness.

Jake looked from one to the other of the brothers. "I know it did. But I'm back now. And I won't pull a disappearing stunt again, I swear."

"As if we care," Daniel muttered.

"That's enough," Shaine said.

"Can it, buddy," Devlin added for good measure.

Daniel pushed back his chair. "I don't want any pie. I'm going to do my homework and go to Art's place. I told him I'd help him with his algebra."

As her son's footsteps stomped up the stairs, Shaine's shoulders sagged. "Let him go, Devlin. What's the use of pretending this is a normal family dinner? It isn't."

"I shouldn't have come," Jake said; he couldn't stand seeing her so careworn. So unhappy.

"Maybe not. But you're here now and we're all having pie," she said. "Connor, would you make the tea? Padric, the pie's in the oven. Devlin, those were great pickles."

"The boy'll get used to the idea that he's got a father," Devlin said. "But it'll take a while."

Encouraged by what sounded like support, Jake said as honestly as he knew how, "I've got the rest of my life. I'm in this for the duration, no matter what it takes."

Devlin made a noncommittal sound. Shaine began serving the pie, while Connor poured tea black as pitch. The pie was excellent. Although he was almost sure bakeapple pie wasn't available anywhere in Manhattan, Jake made no further remarks about New York.

Just as he drained his mug, which had contained enough caffeine to keep him awake for a week, the telephone rang. It was attached to the wall in the kitchen, and as Shaine picked it up, every word was audible. "Cameron," she said with evident pleasure. "How are you?"

Who the hell was Cameron? Jake wondered, his hackles bristling. And what had the man done to deserve that note of intimacy in Shaine's voice?

It had never occurred to Jake to ask her if she was involved with anyone. How was that for stupidity? Or was it just plain egotism?

"You're where?" she continued. "Toronto—why?... They *what?* You really mean it?... In a few days? Oh, Cameron, that's incredible, thanks so much for submitting it... You'll phone as soon as you hear? And how's your mother?... That's good, say hello to her for me. Okay, I'll talk to you soon. 'Bye.''

She put down the receiver and swung to face the four men at the table; her smile was radiant. "That was Cameron," she said unnecessarily. "He submitted one of my panels to a jury in Toronto for a nationwide competition. They're going to let him know next week if I'm accepted for the competition. Right across Canada! Then the winning entry goes to the States."

In the spate of congratulations, Jake sat still. Cameron, he'd gathered, was acting as Shaine's agent. So how did she know Cameron's mother? As Shaine ran upstairs to tell Daniel her news, Jake gathered up the dishes and put them in the sink. He was going to find out, he thought grimly. It was past time he got a few answers. Filling the sink with hot sudsy water, he began washing the glasses.

And there was something in his stance that announced he was planning to outstay the three brothers, no matter how late they hung around.

CHAPTER SIX

WHEN Shaine came back downstairs, her son was trailing behind her. "I'll give you a drive to Art's, Daniel," Devlin said, then asked his brothers, "You guys want a drive, too? See you, Jake."

Within moments Jake and Shaine had the kitchen to themselves. "The fish was superb and I've been to funerals that were more fun than that dinner," Jake said, swishing soap from a dinner plate.

"At least it didn't turn into an all-out brawl."

"It might have if Devlin hadn't been here. He's the one with common sense."

She picked up a plate and began drying it. "He's the eldest. So he's the one who missed Mum and Da the most."

Jake rested a soapy hand on her wrist. "It must have been a terrible time for all of you, Shaine."

"It was." She muttered, polishing the plate until it shone. "Da had driven all the way from Corner Brook and they were within sight of home...it was such a stupid accident."

"You weren't home when it happened."

"I was still at university. Mum and Da insisted I stay there after Daniel was born. Mum was looking after him. But I'd told them the day before on the phone that I couldn't do that anymore—I couldn't bear to be so far away from my son—so I was going to quit my courses and come back to the cove." She stared down at the plate and said in a muffled voice, "I've sometimes wondered if they were worrying about me, so maybe Da's attention wasn't on the road..."

Compassion twisting his gut, Jake took her in his arms,

the plate digging into his ribs. "Black ice can fool the best of drivers," he said forcefully. "You mustn't blame yourself."

"I—I've never told anyone that," she said shakily, realizing in a wave of emotion how safe she felt in his arms; and how comforting it was to share a burden she'd carried alone for so long. "I always could tell you stuff, Jake. For years you were my best friend."

Guilt added itself to compassion. "I keep saying I'm sorry I didn't get in touch. But what does *I'm sorry* mean? Easy words to say, and no way to mend the damage."

"I'm worried about Daniel."

"Let's hope Devlin's right, and in time he'll accept the idea of having a real father on the scene." Very gently Jake stroked her cheek, his fingers feeling rough and clumsy.

She shifted in his arms, no longer feeling so safe. "We'd better finish the dishes."

But Jake tightened his hold, dropping his cheek onto her hair. "You feel so good," he said softly. "So right."

She pushed the plate hard against him. "You mustn't do this to me," she said wildly. "You tear me apart! I can't go to bed with you. I've got a family and gossipy neighbors and this is my home. It's okay for you, you can just leave whenever it suits you. But I can't."

He tilted her chin so her eyes met his; her lashes were spiky with unshed tears. "Don't cry," he said hoarsely. "The first time I saw you, you were crying. It does me in every time."

She jerked free. "I'm not crying on purpose! I can't stand weepy females."

He took one corner of the dish towel and dabbed her eyes. "There," he said with a crooked grin, "that's better."

As though she couldn't help herself, Shaine reached up and traced the faint lines at the corners of his eyes. "You said I'd changed. You have, too. I know you've got a lot of money now and you're a successful man. But I don't think it's always been easy."

Feeling as if something that had frozen hard all those years ago was starting to melt, Jake rasped, "Why did you tell me you didn't love me enough to go away with me? Was it really true, Shaine?"

She stilled in his embrace. Of all the questions he could have asked, it was the one she least wanted to answer. "It was a long time ago—why drag it up now?"

"Because it's important."

"To you, maybe."

"No *maybe* about it."

"I'm not digging up the past when the present's more than I can deal with. Daniel's what's important here. Not your feelings or mine."

"How can we separate our feelings from him? We're his parents, Shaine. You and I."

"You have yet to prove to me that you'll be a real father."

"I've told you I'll hang in!"

"Words are cheap."

She looked as if she could explode like a firecracker. "Heaven help me," Jake said, "I love watching you lose your cool. You do it so well. Flash, flare and sparkle—a class act."

She made a rude noise. "Years of practice with lots of men to practice on. You. Three brothers. A son."

"And who else?" Jake said, his mouth dry. "What about Cameron?"

"Cameron'd be terribly upset if I ever lost my cool with him. Anyway, he's such a nice man I never need to."

"Nice," Jake repeated. "So he's out of the running."

"What do you mean?"

"You'd never settle with someone nice. You'd be bored out of your skull before the honeymoon was over."

"For someone who vanished for thirteen years, you seem to know a lot about me."

"I'm your most appreciative audience," he said, tweaking her hair. "On the rare occasions when I've lost my cool with a woman—rare because I didn't let any of them close enough—she'd run for shelter. But not you. You come out with both fists flying."

"You don't scare me, Jake Reilly."

"Oh, Shaine," he said softly, "you shouldn't say something like that to me."

He took the plate from her, put it on the counter and settled his arms comfortably around her waist. Then he bent his head and pressed his mouth to hers. With exquisite control he moved against her, flicking her lips with his tongue, taking their softness between his teeth and nibbling; and felt her resistance crumble. With all the passion he'd come to expect from her, she looped her hands around his nape, pulled his head down and kissed him back.

He was falling, drowning, sinking into her beauty, her fire, the taut bones and gorgeous curves of her body. Overcome by a desperate hunger, an ache that could be assuaged by only one outcome, Jake dragged his mouth free. Dazzled by the green depths of her irises, the voluptuous red of her mouth, he realized she was trembling all over; the floor seemed to shift under his feet. "Daniel could walk in the door at any time," he muttered. "I can't keep my hands off you."

"You know what?" she said blankly. "I'd forgotten about him. What kind of mother does that make me?"

"How about a woman with needs of her own?"

"I can't afford those needs," she cried. "Jake, go home. Back to your motel. Back to New York or Singapore or wherever it is you hang out."

"I'm in no state to walk out the door."

She flushed scarlet, turned to the sink and plunged her hands in. "My life was nicely in order until you turned up.

The shop's doing well, I love working with glass, Daniel was happy. But now I don't even know which way's up.''

Entranced, Jake said, "Is that what you want on your tombstone? I had an orderly life?" As she thunked a couple of plates into the rack, he added, "Fantasizing about breaking those over my head?"

"It's the other fantasies I can't deal with."

He came up behind her, clasped her by the hips and moved against her as suggestively as he knew how. "Stop!" she gasped. "Or I swear I'll dunk you under the cold tap."

Jake, once again, was in no shape to walk out the door. As for Shaine, she was scouring another plate with vicious energy. Leaving her to it, he wandered into the dining room. He'd already figured out from the layout of the house where Shaine's studio must be located; he wanted to see it. He opened the door that led to a new extension on the house, flicking on the light.

Once again he was face-to-face with her ardent commitment to color. All along one wall hung what he would have called Shaine's bread and butter: the herring gulls, lighthouses, whales and pitcher plants that the tourists would buy by the dozen. But it was the panels placed by the windows that drew him. Whether they were geometric, abstract or realistic, none was without the surprise of genuine originality.

Shaine said irritably, "Who gave you permission to look in here?"

He said with real admiration, "These panels—they're great. You've accomplished an enormous amount, Shaine. Three fine brothers, a loving son, your shop and this. You must've driven yourself as hard as I have."

"Didn't we become friends because we were alike?"

"Alike, and different from all the rest."

Gazing at an oval sunrise, in which sky and water ached with color, he realized how at every turn he was being drawn deeper and deeper into her life. Into the woman she'd become, against the most difficult of odds. He'd had it easy in comparison, Jake thought humbly, because he'd been unencumbered. Free to do what he wanted, when and where and however he wanted to.

What if Daniel never accepted him? Shaine would have no choice but to side with her son.

Everything was moving too fast; he needed breathing space. "I was looking at Daniel's hockey schedule on the refrigerator," he said. "I'll drive into Corner Brook tomorrow and watch his game after school—maybe that'll give him the message that I'm around but I'm not planning on taking over his life. I can stay just over a week—then I've got meetings in New York and Hong Kong. We'll see how it's going by the time I leave."

Shaine asked the crucial question. "What if he's as angry with you then as he is now? Will you come back, Jake?"

He ran his fingers through his hair. "Yeah...I've got a lot of time to make up for. And now I'm going to get out of here. I'll drop by tomorrow and no, I'm not going to kiss you good night because we both know where that'll lead."

She felt suddenly exhausted, and frighteningly vulnerable. Her voice a thin thread, she said, "We should never have made love on the island—what were we thinking of?"

Shaine the fighter challenged him; but Shaine unhappy and discouraged touched Jake in ways he wasn't ready for. "We were young. Thinking wasn't top of the list. And no matter the consequences, I can't bring myself to regret it." Not giving her any quarter, he added, "You wouldn't wish Daniel out of existence, would you?"

Shocked, she said, "No!"

"Well, then. See you sometime tomorrow."

He let himself out into the cool mist. The foghorn on the island wailed through the darkness, hauntingly lonely. A warning, thought Jake. Beware.

*   *   *

At the hockey game in Corner Brook, Jake made himself as unobtrusive as possible; yet, as though he were a magnet, Daniel's eyes flew over the bleachers and picked him out almost instantly. The boy made no gesture of recognition; but he played with a reckless disregard for sense and safety that had Jake's heart in his mouth. He also played brilliantly, and largely due to his efforts his team won by a good margin.

After a tasteless meal at a fast-food outlet, Jake did a little shopping, then drove back to the cove. He'd told Shaine he'd drop in; and knew he'd been delaying doing so all day. He'd even gone to see Maggie and Marty after lunch, spending the better part of an hour dodging Maggie's intrusive questions.

If he visited Shaine now, he'd probably see Daniel.

Was he afraid of his own son?

The fog had retreated during the day. The yellow house with its studio facing the cliffs looked very welcoming, lights on in nearly all the rooms. Jake parked his car and knocked on the back door. Shaine yanked it open, her face white as the surf. "I thought you might be Padric," she gasped.

"Padric? Why?"

"Haven't you heard? I thought that's why you were here."

He stepped in the doorway, putting an arm around her because she looked like she might fall down. "Heard what, Shaine? For God's sake, what's the matter?"

"Padric went hunting early this morning. Said he'd be back midafternoon. He didn't come home, so they're out looking for him."

"It's only been dark a couple of hours...maybe he got a deer and stayed behind to gut it."

"You don't understand," she said frantically. "He was going into Corner Brook with a bunch of his friends to play in a pool championship this evening—the deer isn't born that'd make him late for that."

"Where are they looking?" Jake demanded. "Can you loan me a flashlight?"

"Back of the Mulligans'. There's a trail that goes into Black's Lake, that's where he usually goes."

"Where's Daniel?"

"He hasn't—oh, here he is now."

A van had drawn up on the street. Daniel got out, lugging his gear and stick. When he saw Jake in the doorway, he hesitated in the path. Then he picked up his pace. "You gonna let me in?" he said.

Shaine moved aside. Kissing her son quickly on the cheek, she said, "Padric's lost in the woods. Everyone's out looking for him."

"No way!"

She looked around the porch as though she was the one who was lost. "Flashlight," she muttered, "where is it, Daniel?"

The boy pushed aside a couple of jackets and passed it to her. "I put a new battery in last week. Where's Uncle Dev?"

"Out with one of the search parties."

"I'll go help him look."

"No!" she exclaimed. "You're too young and you've got school tomorrow."

"Mum, that's not—"

"Why doesn't he come with me?" Jake said. "It's one more pair of eyes."

She glared at him. "You're interfering with—"

"I want to go, Mum!"

Shaine's shoulders sagged. "Okay, okay. Jake, will you promise not to let Daniel out of your sight? I said I'd stay here until they find Padric, they'll let me know as soon as they hear anything."

"Yep. You hear that, kid? You've got to swear you won't take off on me."

Daniel scowled at him. "I'll change into my boots," he said, "and grab a sweater."

"Daniel," Jake said quietly, "you're not going anywhere until you answer me."

Daniel's blue eyes, full of defiance, clashed with Jake's. Jake had no intention of backing down; if he did, he'd lose any chance of gaining the boy's respect. Grudgingly, Daniel said, "Okay. I'll stick with you."

"Good. My boots are in the car, I'll wait for you there." Jake gave Shaine a quick, hard hug. "Padric'll be back in his own bed by midnight—try not to worry."

Shortly afterward he and Daniel were driving away from the yellow house. At Mulligans', a long row of cars and trucks had parked in the field. A ranger with a two-way radio was standing beside his van. "What's up?" Jake asked.

"Nothing yet. They've combed the lakeshore and Corkum's Hills, that's the best deer country 'round here. So now one batch is heading west of there, and one north. You know these woods?"

"I grew up here," Jake said absently, "I know them like the back of my hand. There's a place I used to go where I always saw deer, it's east of the lake." He bent over the map spread on the hood of the truck. "Here. Daniel and I'll head that way. It'll take us a couple of hours to check the whole area."

"The fire station'll blow the alarm when he's found. You'll hear that even way off in the woods."

"Okay, Daniel?" Jake asked. "This could be a total waste of time, you understand that?"

As the boy nodded, Jake set off across the field, moving at a smooth clip he could keep up for hours. He said little, occasionally pointing out a landmark on the way, and making sure they stopped to drink water every so often. In the years he'd been away, the trees had grown and the under-growth had sprouted high; but he still knew every rise and fall of the ground, every granite outcrop and swamp. "There was a cave," he said to his son. "I used to sneak out there and smoke when I was your age...I had no more sense than a beached whale. I never showed the place to anyone else, so it's a long shot that Padric would have found it."

Daniel grunted. Jake gave an inner sigh. He'd hoped that walking through the forest at night might loosen his son's tongue. "Another half a mile," he said, and concentrated on picking his way over the roots of spruce and fir. These were his roots, he thought. Literally. He shouldn't have stayed away so long, cutting himself off from such a vital part of his own history.

If he'd come back sooner, he'd have found out about Daniel sooner.

Remorse slammed through him, with its sense of irre-trievable loss. He could have known Daniel at five, or seven, or nine, and maybe been accepted wholeheartedly. But he'd been too goddamned stubborn to come home.

The boughs brushing his sleeve, the overhead arch of maples and beech shutting out the stars felt claustrophobic. Shining the flashlight ahead, he picked out the stream bed that was the last climb before they came to the cave. "Not long now," he said over his shoulder. "You're in good shape for someone who played hockey this afternoon as if the devil was on his tail."

Daniel heaved himself up the slope and said nothing. Jake stopped at the top of the hill and shouted as loudly as he could, "Padric!"

A startled bird flailed through the trees. Jake yelled again, cupping his hands to magnify his voice. Very faintly, he heard someone groan. "Daniel, did you hear that?"

"Right ahead of us."

"That's where the cave is. Let's go."

New energy racing through his body, Jake led the way. Witherod and high-bush cranberry had overgrown the mouth of the cave; but the beam of his flashlight picked out a couple of broken branches. "Padric," he shouted again.

"Near the cave," Padric wavered.

Jake reached a helping hand behind him and hauled Daniel up the steep rocks. Then he saw the plaid of Padric's shirt and the pale gleam of his face. Padric was awkwardly sprawled among the rocks, one leg bent beneath him. Jake dropped to his knees. "What happened?"

"Fell on the rocks," Padric gasped; his face was haggard and he was obviously in pain. "Damn fool thing to do. Bust my shinbone."

"Give him some water, Daniel," Jake said, thinking fast. "I know I promised your mum I wasn't going to let you out of my sight—but will you stay with Padric while I go for help?"

"Sure," Daniel said. "Mum put some cookies and fruit in my pack. Want some, Uncle Padric?"

"She didn't put a beer in, did she?" Padric grinned.

"I'm under age, not allowed near it," Daniel said with a matching grin.

Wishing with all his heart that Daniel would just once turn that smile on him, Jake said, "I'll be back as soon as I can. Probably be a couple of hours, though, by the time we get a stretcher and medical help."

"How did you know where to look?" Padric asked.

"I always saw deer out here when I was a kid. Kept it secret, though. But it seemed like the kind of place you'd find."

"Thanks, buddy," Padric said quietly. "Not my idea of a good time to spend the night out here."

"My pleasure," Jake said sincerely. "See you later."

It was just under two hours when he and a couple of paramedics labored up the slope to the cave. Jake was lead-ing the way again, and in a quick glance saw that Daniel had fallen asleep, his head resting on Padric's chest. Jake stopped in his tracks, his heart turning over with love for the boy. Padric said weakly, his gray eyes trained on Jake's face, "I figured you'd fly south like the geese before you'd turn into a real father, Jake. But I reckon I was wrong."

"Thanks, Padric," Jake said huskily.

"Remember you said I should ask Shaine why you left all those years ago? She told me flat-out to back off."

Jake laughed. "That's Shaine for you."

"Anyone who could sit through that dinner isn't going to give up easy," Padric muttered. "The kid's worth waiting for. He's a good kid."

"I know that," Jake said, and as the team clambered up the rocks, watched Daniel wake up, stretching and rubbing his eyes.

The next hour was arduous, and despite painkillers must have been agonizing for Padric. Daniel walked beside the stretcher as much as he could, his uncle's hand locked in his. When they reached the field, Jake saw that Shaine was waiting beside the warden's truck; she was dressed in jeans, a wool shirt and a down vest.

She began running when she saw them, and fell to her knees beside the stretcher. "Padric, are you all right? I was so relieved when they phoned—I was afraid they'd never find you."

"Slipped on the moss. Broke my shinbone," Padric said.

"You stupid idiot," she quavered. "Going off and not telling anyone where you were going. If it wasn't for Jake, you'd still be out there. Oh, Padric, I'm so glad you're safe, don't ever do that to me again."

Over her shoulder, as she wept into his chest, Padric winked at Jake. Patting his sister on the back, he mumbled, "Get off me, girl, I need a doctor and a good drink of rum."

Shaine surged to her feet and flung her arms around Jake.

"How can I ever thank you?" she sobbed. "I was worried sick, I was nearly out of my mind by the time they called to say you'd found him."

She filled his embrace beautifully, her body soft and warm and infinitely desirable. But—apart from Daniel, who had studiously turned away—they had a very gratified audience. Jake said in a strangled voice, "Glad I could help."

She whirled. "Daniel, are you okay?"

"Yeah, Mum, I'm fine."

"There's an ambulance waiting," she said. "Jake, will you stay with Daniel if I go to the hospital with Padric? He'll have to have X-rays in Corner Brook."

"I can go to Uncle Dev's place," Daniel said.

"They're not back yet…Jake?"

As Jake nodded, Padric said in a resigned voice, "I bet our team's been disqualified from the championship."

"That's the least of your worries," Shaine said roundly. "Good, here comes Doc McGillivray."

Jake glanced up. The man padding into the circle of light had gained a little weight over the years, his hair grizzled but just as flyaway as it had always been, his eyebrows like two hedges. "Hello, Doc," Jake said.

Doc's attention had been on the man on the stretcher. His eyes skewed to meet Jake's. "Jake Reilly," he said in an unreadable voice. "I didn't know you were in these parts."

"Then you must be the only person who didn't," Jake said easily. But he was puzzled; he'd have sworn that Doc's initial reaction on seeing him had been guilt rather than pleasure. Guilt? What for? He added, "I'll drop by for a visit in the next couple of days."

"You do that," Doc said, overheartily. "Now then, Padric, what have you been doing to yourself?"

Without fuss he gave Padric an injection against the pain, then the little cavalcade paced across the field toward the flashing yellow lights of the ambulance. Before she climbed in through the back doors, Shaine looped her arms around Jake's neck. "Thank you, thank you," she breathed. "I couldn't bear to think of him out in the woods all night."

Wishing everyone else ten miles away, Jake said with manful restraint, "You're welcome."

She followed the stretcher into the ambulance, which bumped away toward the road. Gratitude was all very well, Jake thought. But he wanted a lot more than gratitude from Shaine.

What exactly did he want?

Shaine, accompanied by Devlin and Connor, arrived back at the house about three in the morning; Padric had a broken tibia, and was being kept overnight. Daniel, so Jake reported to Shaine, had gone to bed the minute they'd got back to the house. Without saying as much as a word to his father; but Jake kept that to himself.

After receiving gruffly spoken thanks from Padric's two brothers, Jake left as soon as he could. He slept late the next morning, listened to the weather forecast, perfected his plan in his mind and made several phone calls. Promptly at nine-thirty the following day, he walked into The Fin Whale Craft Shop. Shaine's assistant, a pretty young woman named Jenny, gave him a conspiratorial smile. "Shaine's in the back room, packing orders," she said.

"Thanks," Jake said, and pushed through the door.

Shaine looked up. For a moment pure pleasure flashed across her face. Then she said repressively, "I'm busy, Jake."

She looked neither grateful nor lustful. Jake said cheerfully, taking the box from her and putting it on the floor, "Not so busy that you're not coming with me."

She frowned at him. "I'm not going anywhere with you."

He kicked the door shut behind him with one foot. "You

don't want the whole shop hearing us argue. My car's out-side and I've got everything we'll need.''

''Telling people what to do might work in the board-room—but this isn't New York.''

''You're so right. Are you coming willingly, or do I have to pick you up and carry you?''

''Stop making fun of me!''

In a single swift movement Jake lifted her into his arms and pried the door open again. Two customers had come into the store; luckily neither one was Maggie. Shaine said in a furious undertone, ''Put me down.''

''It's an unfair world—I'm bigger and stronger than you,'' he said, walking across the room. ''Hi, there, Mrs. Mulligan, nice to see you. Fair bit of excitement a couple of nights ago, wasn't it? 'Bye, Jenny. Thanks.''

The bell rang sweetly as he walked outside. His car was parked at the curb. ''I can't leave Jenny all day,'' Shaine protested.

''Yes, you can—I checked with her yesterday. She's packed a lunch for herself and she'll lock up at six. And Daniel's gone to St. Anthony to play hockey.''

Dumping Shaine unceremoniously on the road, but keep-ing a tight arm around her waist, Jake opened the passenger door. ''Hop in.''

''What are you doing, kidnapping me?''

''You bet.''

Her eyes narrowed. ''I am not going to bed with you.''

''We're not going anywhere near a bed,'' he said truth-fully. ''Believe me, when the time comes for you and me to make love, I won't have to kidnap you.''

Her eyes flashed green. ''I must be the stupidest woman this side of Cape Spear. You're behaving like a Neanderthal and my hormones are on a rampage.''

''You're so good for my ego,'' Jake said. ''Sit, Shaine.''

She plunked herself down on the seat. ''I am not your

pet poodle! You do realize this little escapade will be all over the village by lunchtime?''

"We won't be here to hear it," he said, and slid behind the wheel. He drove straight to the wharf, where he parked by the side of the road. "I have clothes in the back for you, and a picnic lunch. Let's go."

She bit her lip; amusement, he was pleased to see, was now lurking in her eyes. "It's a very beautiful day," she said.

"Ordered specially for you."

"You're rude and overbearing."

"Sexy, though. According to you."

He had that right. "I have to be home at three," she said triumphantly, "to stay with Padric."

"No, you don't. Devlin's going to."

"So is the whole village in on this little conspiracy?"

"Would I do that to you?" Jake said piously. "Want to grab that bag?"

Tom Banks, one of Jake's father's fishing partners, was striding up the wharf toward them. He tipped his cap to Shaine. "Boat's all set to go, boy," he said to Jake. "Don't need to tell you how to run 'er, do I?"

"Some things you don't forget, Tom."

Sun was sparkling on the water, and waves slapped at the wooden wharf. Jake inhaled with huge delight. "Diesel fuel, rotting bait and salt water—is there anything better?"

The wind flirting with her skirt, Shaine said, "I haven't been out in a boat for two or three years."

"Then we'll fix that right away," Jake said. After helping her down the ladder, he passed her the bags and picnic hamper. Then he jumped down, and as Tom untied the hawsers and tossed them to the deck, he turned the key, listening to the engine catch and settle into a smooth purr. "You always did know how to baby an engine, Tom," he yelled. "Thanks, we'll be back by four."

In a smooth curve, *Gertrude* pulled away from the wharf.

Shaine disappeared into the cabin, appearing a few minutes later in green shorts and a flowered shirt, her pretty sandals replaced by rubber-soled shoes. She gave Jake a smile of uncomplicated pleasure and sat on the thwart, trailing her fingers in the bow wave. Jake smiled back. His legs had adjusted automatically to the sway of the waves, and the helm fit his palm perfectly. That Shaine was with him added the final touch to his happiness.

When had he last felt so carefree?

CHAPTER SEVEN

GHOST ISLAND was half an hour offshore. As the village diminished behind the boat, herring gulls wheeled overhead, impossibly white against the deep blue of the sky. Jake wasn't sure how Shaine would react when she realized the island was their destination; he'd soon find out. As he steered toward the jetty, then nudged *Gertrude* against the rough wooden boards, Shaine neatly looped a hawser over a protruding pylon. She scrambled onto the jetty, holding the rope taut.

Jake turned off the motor. "They must have repaired the jetty."

"A couple of years ago," she replied, taking the hamper from him. As he joined her on the jetty, she said forthrightly, "I've never been back here, Jake. Not once."

"Then I'm glad you've come back with me," he said, and watched her lashes flutter to hide her eyes. "I brought a couple of pails, thought we might find some late bakeapples. Or crowberries."

There was, briefly but unmistakably, relief on her face. He said roughly, "Shaine, I didn't bring you out here to seduce you. I just thought we needed a day away from everyone. Away from the village and our son and your brothers."

"Two friends picking berries."

It wasn't quite that simple. "Yeah," said Jake.

In companionable silence, they picked the small orange fruit for nearly two hours. Then Shaine straightened, stretching her back. "I'm hungry."

"Then let's eat."

The motel restaurant had packed the hamper. "Chicken

sandwiches,'' Shaine said contentedly, helping herself. "They always were your favorite. And I love any food I don't make myself.''

He poured her a glass of chilled white wine, and passed carrot and celery sticks. It was an unsophisticated meal that many of his clients would have decried; but to Jake, seated on a rock surrounded by ocean and with Shaine just two feet away, it was ambrosia.

She said abruptly, "Your dad drowned off this island.''

"Near the reef by the lighthouse.''

"Someone told me your mother had remarried.''

"Several years ago.'' Briefly he described his stepfather. "She's happy again. After Dad died, she couldn't bear looking out her window every day and seeing the ocean that had killed him. So she left, and broke all her ties with the village. One more reason I didn't know about Daniel.''

"You never even wrote me one letter,'' Shaine said quietly, making no attempt to hide that old sense of betrayal.

He wasn't quite ready to go there yet. "I should never have stayed away those thirteen years. Walking through the woods the other night, being out on the ocean today... they're part of me, a part I'd lost. When I left here after we'd made love, I drove myself unmercifully. Worked on freighters and salvage rigs, salted away my money, then started playing the stock market. I always was a mathematical whiz. I took some appalling chances, and enough of them paid off that I made a lot of money rather too fast. The more I had, the harder I played. I found my first two or three private clients, the only stipulation being that they had to be comfortable with a high level of risk for high returns. My name got around by word of mouth, and some big names came on board. I haven't looked back since.''

She said naively, "Are you very rich?''

"Very,'' he said. "I own two places in New York, a ski chalet in the Swiss Alps and a flat in Paris, within walking distance of the Louvre. You'd like it there.'' As longing rippled over her face, he added, "But even before I came back here a couple of weeks ago, I was starting to see that along the way I've lost something. My soul? That's a hell of a big word."

Shaine passed him another sandwich, her eyes on his face. He said ruefully, "I'd forgotten what a good listener you are—I didn't mean to bore you."

"You're not."

"There's a gap in my life," he burst out. "A hollow place, which no amount of money can fill." Gazing down at the food in his hand as though he'd never seen a chicken sandwich before, he added, "Then I find out about Daniel. And I see you again."

"I'm not the same person I was thirteen years ago."

"I've asked you this before—did you mean what you said that last day? That you didn't love me enough to go away with me? It wasn't like you, Shaine—you never were someone to do things by half measures, and you'd told me often enough you loved me."

She said, with a faint, reminiscent smile, "We were planning to share your apartment in Manhattan, weren't we? I was going to take art courses and find a studio. My parents would have preferred something more conservative—they wanted me to enroll in university—but they were willing for me to go because they trusted you."

"But you didn't go."

"There was a reason I couldn't go with you," Shaine said carefully. "A very real reason. But I couldn't tell you about it at the time, I'd promised I wouldn't. Not that it would have made any difference in the long run."

He put all the force of his personality into his words. "I want you to tell me now."

"Do you remember being here that day?"

"I've never forgotten the smallest detail."

She flinched. "You kept on and on at me, begging, pleading, trying so hard to make me change my mind...the truth was, I was as desperate for wider horizons as you were.''

With the tenacity of a bulldog, Jake brought her back to the point. ''What was the reason?''

''Doc McGillivray,'' she said. ''I don't imagine you've forgotten how every year, on the anniversary of his wife's death, Doc goes on a bender. Drinks himself silly one day, suffers through the hangover the next, goes back to work on the following day. All the villagers know that 362 days a year he's the best doctor the length of the coast…and if anything happens on the other three, they go into Corner Brook. It's the way it's always been.''

''He looked guilty when he saw me the other night,'' Jake said slowly.

''You see too much.'' She gave a heavy sigh. ''I always visit him on the anniversary, I feel sorry for him because his wife was a lovely woman and he still misses her dreadfully. When I went that year—it was the day before you and I came out here—he let it drop that my mother had cancer. He'd just gotten the reports from Corner Brook; my mother didn't know yet. She'd need surgery, he said, and radiation. Maybe even chemo. He thought the prognosis was good, but it could be months before we'd know for certain whether she'd pull through. Then he suddenly realized he'd said something that should have been kept strictly confidential, so he made me swear not to breathe a word to anyone until after my mother's appointment with him later that week.''

She shrugged. ''That's it. I couldn't possibly leave the cove knowing that my mother would be going through such an ordeal within a matter of weeks. But I couldn't tell you the truth.''

Jake sat very still. Of all the many reasons he'd conjured in his mind over the years, this had never been one of them. Then he realized Shaine was still speaking. ''Technically,

I could have told you once my mother knew, there'd have been no need for secrecy then."

"For the sake of two or three days, we lost thirteen years?" Jake said, appalled.

"But it wasn't just a question of those two or three days," Shaine said passionately. "You're a decent man, Jake, you'd have stayed behind in the cove if you'd found out about my mother. That would have been so wrong for you. Your destiny wasn't in Cranberry Cove, I knew that better than anyone—you'd have gone crazy hanging around here. Worse, you'd have ended up hating me."

"I ended up hating you anyway."

Her lashes flickered. "So I decided before we left in the boat that day to keep my mother's illness a secret as long as I could, and to tell you I didn't love you enough to go away with you. That way, you'd leave for New York without me."

Of all the emotions churning in his chest, relief was uppermost. Jake clasped her by the elbows, his smile irradiating his face. "So you did love me," he said. "You were lying to me just to make me leave."

She pulled away from him, chewing on her lip. "We were so young," she said in a rush. "And I, at least, so naive. So inexperienced. What did we know about love? Country and western songs, the love poems we had to study in high school—what did they have to do with two kids who'd grown up misfits in an out-of-the-way fishing village? We were in love with love, Jake."

"Speak for yourself," Jake said harshly. "I loved you with all my heart. I was young, yes, and not nearly as experienced as you might think. But I knew you were the woman for me."

With huge bitterness she said, "Oh sure. If I meant so much to you, why didn't you write to me or phone me and keep in touch?"

He leaned forward. "Don't you understand? That's precisely why I didn't keep in touch! I couldn't bear to. You didn't love me, that's what you said. So I ran away and hid and spent a very long time licking my wounds. Hell, Shaine, I can see now that I shouldn't have reacted that way. But I was only twenty-two, and here on this island I'd given you my heart.''

"You didn't even say goodbye."

"I couldn't," he said tautly. "I went home, packed my gear and left."

Her hands were twisting in her lap, her head downbent; he had no idea what she was thinking. Raking his fingers through his hair, he added, "I'm not trying to justify it. I'm just telling you the way it was."

"When I told you I wouldn't go away with you, I never thought you'd vanish from my life. We were friends! Didn't that mean anything to you?"

"How could I separate love from friendship? From my perspective you'd rejected me—all of me, my love, my friendship, the works. I was supposed to write you letters talking about the weather? I don't think so."

Her chin set stubbornly, she said, "It doesn't really matter now, does it? My mother had the surgery and radiation, came through in fine style, and then she and Da were killed in a stupid accident. So if I'd gone with you to New York, I would have had to come home to look after my three brothers." She lifted burning eyes. "Would you have come back with me?"

He owed her an honest answer. "I would have, yes. Because I loved you."

"You see? I was right to send you away."

"You made a decision for both of us—you don't think you overstepped your limits?"

"No," she said, her chin high. "I did what was best."

"For you, maybe. But what about Daniel? And me? I appear out of the blue after thirteen years and my own son can't stand the sight of me."

"He'll accept you, given time," she insisted, hoping with all her heart that she was right. "Patience never was your strong suit."

"Nor yours. And don't argue."

"Whatever we do," she said urgently, "we mustn't argue over Daniel."

"We won't," he said shortly. She was so passionately intense; yet in the last few minutes she'd reiterated that she'd never really loved him. Would he ever understand her?

"You were the only real friend I had while I was growing up," Shaine said. "I'd like us to be friends again."

"Friends who want to go to bed with each other? That's what we did wrong the first time."

"You fell in love with me—that was the real mistake."

She was glaring at him as though he was the enemy. His gut clenched as another thought struck him. "Is that why you made love to me—because you were upset about your mother?"

"I made love to you because I'd wanted to tear the clothes off your back ever since you came home for your father's funeral."

"So you lusted after me. Even if you didn't love me," he said bitterly, and in the distance heard a gull scream from the cliffs.

"Why do you have to analyze everything?" she cried.

Unable to stand how beautiful she looked, her back to the sea, sunlight dancing in her hair and bathing her cheek with golden light, he said, "I'm a mathematician—analytical and cold-blooded."

Her nostrils flared. "Would you try and steal Daniel from me by using your money and your power?"

"I've already told you that's not on the cards."

"Then you're not cold-blooded," Shaine said. "I've watched you with Daniel, it hurts you when he's so aloof."

She tossed her head. "And you're not remotely cold-blooded when you kiss me."

He told the literal truth. "Making love with you on this island—nothing in my life has ever matched that, Shaine."

She'd seen the glossy photos in the magazines: the elegant, couturier-clad women with their diamonds and their sheen of assurance. Yet Jake was saying that she, Shaine O'Sullivan of Cranberry Cove, more than equaled them.

"You don't believe me, do you?" Jake said curtly.

"I don't know what I believe!"

As though history was replaying itself, he felt the old hurt lance his ribs. Was he in danger of having his heart broken twice by the same woman? That would be a damn fool thing to do. "Let's go down by the rocks," he said tersely. "Crowberries used to grow down there."

But as Jake reached for an empty bucket, she bent to pick up the same one. Their hands touched, her nails brushing the dark hair on his wrist. With a muffled groan he pushed her down on the grass, fell on top of her and kissed her.

Her tongue slid enticingly along his lips, her breasts were pressed into his ribs, her hips pinned to the ground by his weight. Fire streaked through Jake's veins, and it would have been all too easy to have lost his control in a glorious explosion of desire. But at some deep level, he didn't want to do that. He reared up on one elbow, his eyes running over her flushed face as if he were seeing it for the first time. With one finger he very slowly traced the arc of her brow, the rise and hollow of cheekbone, the sensual curve of her lower lip. "Each time I see you," he said, "your beauty confounds me."

A sudden sheen of tears made Shaine's irises gleam like emeralds. "When you look at me like that, I can scarcely breathe," she said helplessly. She cupped his face in her palms, pulling it down until her lips touched his in a kiss as tentative and exploratory as a young girl's.

Wondering if she could hear the heavy thud of his heart, Jake teased her mouth open, tasting the sweetness that was Shaine, his fingers buried in her molten curls. Then, of its own volition, one of his hands wandered the slim length of her throat, paused to feel the race of her pulse, and pushed aside the collar of her shirt to trace the slender bridge of her collarbone and the delicate hollow beneath it. Her skin was silken-smooth, warm from the sun; she smelled of grass and the ocean. And she was willing: achingly, deliciously willing.

Very deliberately, she undid the first button on her blouse. Then she slid one hand beneath his T-shirt, tangling her fingers in his body hair, where the rippled muscles of his belly clenched to her touch. Fighting for restraint, Jake undid the second button, then the third, brushing her nipples until they were hard as unripe berries. She arched toward him, moaning his name, her eyes darkening. Finding the clasp of her bra between her breasts, Jake undid it and swooped to suckle her. She cried out with pleasure, a cry as wild as a falcon's.

As he thrust between her thighs with his erection, she hauled at his shirt. He tugged it over his head and opened the rest of her blouse, dipping to taste the ivory concavity of her belly. With fierce hunger he reached for her zipper, pushed aside her lacy underwear, and cupped her. She was warm, moist and writhing to his touch in a way that inflamed him. His gaze trained on the gathering storm in her face, he teased her flesh open and with hypnotic certainty took her to the very center of the storm.

Panting, throbbing and his. His, he thought. Only his.

She reached for the waistband of his shorts. "I want you inside me," she gasped. "Now, Jake, now..."

He was aching to be clasped by her in that most primitive of ways. With all his strength he flung himself sideways. "We can't," he gasped. "I don't have anything to protect you against pregnancy. And I bet you don't, either."

Her face was a study of conflicting emotions. "No, I don't."

"We can't risk a repeat. That's one risk I won't take."

Appalled, she muttered, "I never even thought about protection—I must be out of my mind. What is it about you? I'm normally sensible when it comes to things like that."

He'd tumbled from ecstasy to reality too quickly. He said nastily, "With all your other lovers?"

Her laugh was strangled. "Haven't you noticed them— lined up from the back door all the way to Port aux Basques? Have a heart, Jake."

His fingers clamped around her wrist. "Have you really been celibate for years?"

"Yes."

"Why? And don't do the all-men-are-jerks routine."

"I'm too frustrated to come up with any kind of routine," she said furiously. "My sex life—or lack of it—is my business."

So she was still keeping secrets from him. Striving to control his breathing, Jake said, "I purposely didn't bring any protection with me. It's too soon for you and me to fall into bed. Sure, one kiss and we go off like a couple of firecrackers—so what?"

"I'm flattered," she snapped.

"Dammit, Shaine, this time I'm trying to do the right thing."

With fingers that were trembling, she clasped her bra and did up her blouse. Then she tossed him his T-shirt. "Put it on," she ordered, "because—total idiot that I am—I still want to jump your bones."

"My turn to be flattered?" he mocked; and knew he was doing his level best to bring himself back from the brink of something momentous. He'd been the one calling the shots in the affairs he'd had over the years. But Shaine just had to look at him and he was lost. Putty in her hands. Dead in the water. And how was that for mixed metaphors?

"Crowberries," she said with determination. "Come on, we can fill a pail before we leave."

So they trailed down to the rocks and bent to the task of gathering the small, shiny black berries in their fragrant carpet of needle-like green leaves. But for Jake, the ease was gone and the task mechanical. He was glad when the pail was full and they were tramping across the grass toward *Gertrude* and the jetty. He felt as cranky as a rutting moose, he decided, helping Shaine load their gear into the boat before casting off.

Back on the mainland, he carried the berries to Shaine's back door and refused her polite invitation to come in. Daniel would be home from school shortly; he'd had enough emotional ups and downs for one day. He drove back to the motel, took a shower and lay on the bed, flipping through the channels on the TV. Shaine had never really loved him and his son couldn't stand the sight of him. For a man with more dollars in the bank than starfish in the ocean, he wasn't doing too well.

At two on Monday afternoon, Jake arrived at Doc's office; and saw, with a lurch of his heart, Shaine walking away from the office down a path lined with straggly petunias. She got in her car and drove away without seeing him. No use asking Doc what she'd been there for; for 362 days a year, Doc was as close-mouthed as a clam. Five minutes later, Jake was ushered into the office.

"Jake," said Doc, and shook his hand. "Is this visit medical or personal?"

"Personal," Jake said. A photo of Doc's long-dead wife sat on the oak desk. With genuine curiosity he asked, "You've never loved another woman, have you?"

"No. Likely never will."

"I know what happened thirteen years ago. About

Shaine's mother, and how you told Shaine about the surgery. Do you think Shaine loved me back then?''

''She got into bed with you. Daniel's the proof of that.''

''Come clean, Doc.''

''You still in love with her?''

''If I had the answer to that, I probably wouldn't be here.''

Doc toyed with his stethoscope. ''She worshiped the ground you walked on. Did ever since she was nine or ten.''

''Still did at eighteen?''

''What do you think?''

''At the risk of sounding conceited, I'd have said yes. But she claims it was all about adolescent romance and sappy songs.''

''I'm really sorry I told her what I did,'' Doc said roughly. ''It was inexcusable, and inadvertently I changed your life. But you know, Jake, she would have come home when her mother and father died...and you being the kind of man you are, why, you'd have come with her. It would have half killed you to be back in the cove, it was never big enough for you. You'd have ended up resenting her and her brothers, and perhaps even your own son.''

''Daniel won't pass the time of day with me.''

''Daniel's been looking for you all his life. But he's stubborn like his old man, and not about to admit he might need something from you.''

''You expect me to believe that?''

''You're wasting your time and mine if you don't.''

''When are you going to leave family practice for psychiatry?'' Jake countered sardonically.

''You think there's a difference?'' Doc knit his bushy white brows. ''Listen to me, Jake, and then I'm going to shut up. Shaine's champing at the bit to get out of this place. But she can't because of Daniel. Or so she thinks. Why don't you work on that angle? You're a smart man, if you can make a million bucks you can figure out how to spring the two of them from Cranberry Cove. Now off you go and good luck to you.''

Jake, who could terrorize CEOs with one look, left. Wasn't Doc advising him to use his much-vaunted brain? To quit worrying about love and focus on practicalities? Thoughtfully he got in his car and drove to Shaine's shop, only to discover from Jenny that Shaine was home working in her studio. On the steps of the yellow house, Jake tapped on the door and walked in. The kitchen counter was a jumble of unwashed dishes. He knocked just as perfunctorily on the studio door. Pushing it open, he said, ''Hi, Shaine.''

Wearing an oversize canvas apron, she was bent over her worktable, a hammer in one hand, a flat-edged nail in the other. A design was taking place, he saw with interest, the table littered with numbered pieces of precut colored glass and strips of what looked like lead. He pulled up a stool and sat down. ''Keep working,'' he said amiably.

''Just make yourself at home.''

''Sarcasm doesn't become you. What are the nails for?''

''They're horseshoe nails. They keep the pieces of glass tightly in place,'' she said, selecting a prestretched length of lead came and cutting it with the curved blade of her knife. ''Daniel has hockey at five.''

''We can go together,'' he said. ''How's Padric?''

''Driving everyone nuts—he hates sitting still. It's all around the village that Daniel's father's back in town.''

''Hell,'' Jake said succinctly.

She worked the lead into a curve of red glass. ''I've been asked three times today when we're getting married.''

Jake raised his brow. ''What did you say?''

''I said you hadn't asked me to marry you.''

''Will you marry me, Shaine?''

Her finger slipped, and to his dismay he saw a bright drop of blood blossom on her skin. She got up, ran water over her finger in the sink, then stuck on a Band-Aid. ''You don't want to fool around with lead poisoning,'' she said casually, ''and no, I won't.''

''Lead poisoning?'' he repeated, horrified.

''I take all the precautions, Jake.'' She sat down and selected the next piece of glass, placing it on the paper pattern, then grozing it with a pair of pliers to make a perfect fit. Tiny shards of glass fell to the table.

''I begin to see why you have scars on your fingers,'' Jake remarked. ''Why won't you marry me?''

Her eyes shot green fire. ''I have a son. Or had you forgotten? Cranberry Cove is where we live, where he plays hockey and goes to school. Not New York or Paris.''

''Would you like to live in New York?''

She put down the hammer, letting all the pent-up frustration of years color her voice. ''I'll say this once and only once. I'd give everything I own to live anywhere but here. But it's not possible until Daniel's eighteen, so there's no point in talking about it.''

''What would you do in New York that you can't do here?''

''Are you serious?'' She ticked off her fingers. ''Have access to a kiln. Learn how to paint on glass, and etch with sand and acids. Visit other artists' studios, talk to people who'd understand what I'm so desperate to learn. Go to galleries. Study. Expand. Take risks. Grow.''

Her voice was trembling with the strength of her feelings. ''Lots of kids live in New York and Paris,'' Jake said.

''Daniel's lived here all his life. His friends are here, his uncles, his hockey team. I can't take him away from everything that's familiar for my own selfish reasons, it wouldn't be right.'' Aimlessly she stared at the pliers. ''It's just that I get so tired of waiting. And if you say one word to Daniel about this, I'll take my glass cutter and carve you into enough little pieces to make a mosaic.''

So Doc had been right, Jake thought. Shaine was desperate to leave and couldn't because of Daniel. Was it up to him, Jake, to do something about that?

It seemed to him it could be.

CHAPTER EIGHT

THROUGH the studio door, which Jake had left ajar, came a musical, four-note chiming. "Darn," Shaine said, "there's the doorbell. The front door," she added, looking a little puzzled. "No one ever comes to the front door. I'll be right back."

As she disappeared into the living room, Jake shamelessly followed her. A man was standing on the front step, wearing knife-sharp gray flannels and a navy-blue blazer with a crest on the pocket. He was a nice-looking man, not a hair out of place, his teeth a testament to an orthodontist's skills. Jake wasn't at all surprised when Shaine said, "Cameron! What are you doing here? Come in."

Cameron leaned forward and kissed her sedately on the cheek. "I was in St. John's at a gallery, and decided to make a detour," he said. "I have good news for you."

As she closed the door behind him, Jake eased back into the shadows. St. John's was over 500 miles from Cranberry Cove; it wasn't his idea of a detour. "News about the competition?" Shaine asked.

"Your panel was accepted."

"It was? Oh, Cameron, that's wonderful!" She danced a little jig on the carpet. "I can't thank you enough for entering that panel, it's my favorite of all the work I did last year. But now I'll have to wait two months for the judges to decide...that's forever."

"I think you have a very good chance of placing well," Cameron said, smiling at her, "that's why I entered your work."

The man's head over heels in love with her, Jake

113

thought, cleared his throat and stepped into the living room. "Why don't you introduce me to your friend, Shaine?"

If he'd expected her to be disconcerted, he was out of luck. "Cameron," she said smoothly, "this is Jake Reilly. I'll tell you now because everyone from Labrador to the Grand Banks is in on the secret—Jake is Daniel's father. He's on a short visit from New York."

Jake pumped Cameron's hand vigorously. "Nice to meet you," he said. "I'm glad you've been looking after Shaine's business interests—she's very good, isn't she? Having her name on your roster will certainly add to your reputation."

Cameron said stiffly, "Shaine and I have known each other for three years. We're very good friends, Mr. Reilly."

Not good enough for Shaine to abandon celibacy. "I'm sure you are. Shaine needs contact with the outside world."

Shaine shot him a fulminating glance, then turned back to Cameron. "How long can you stay?"

"Only until tomorrow. I have a flight to Toronto in the afternoon."

"I'll make up the bed in the guest room," she said warmly. "Only thing is, I have to go to Daniel's hockey game later on, it's a semifinal and I promised him I'd be there." Her brow crinkled. "Not your thing, I know."

Cameron said gallantly, "I'd be delighted to go with you."

"That's sweet of you," Shaine said, patting him on the sleeve. "Why don't you bring your bag in, and I'll make you some herbal tea."

As Cameron obediently walked toward his car, she whirled. "How dare you insult him, Jake?"

"He's not the man for you and never will be."

"Why don't you let me decide that? Cameron's a fine man who's utterly dependable. He's stood by me. Which is more than you've done."

Her instinct for his vulnerable spots was unerring. "But he doesn't make your hormones shoot off the chart."

"There's more to life than sex."

"Keep your voice down," Jake said lazily, "you wouldn't want to shock Cameron." He kissed her firmly on the lips. "I'll see you at the rink." Then he strode down the path, saying an amiable goodbye to Cameron as he went.

Jake's lean, rangy build, the unconscious grace with which he moved: for a minute Shaine was catapulted back in time, to his final game at the rink the year he'd graduated from high school. He'd scored the winning goal in the last ten seconds against the school's arch rivals and the arena had gone wild. Including her and all the other thirteen-year-old girls who'd been screaming their heads off during all three periods. As he'd come off the ice, Jake had seen her there, grinned at her and kissed her lightly on the cheek. The other girls had looked at her with huge respect. Whereas she'd lived on the memory of that kiss for the whole five years he'd been at university...

"Shaine?" Cameron said frostily.

She flushed. "Sorry," she mumbled, and led him into the house. There was no risk involved in inviting Cameron to stay overnight. Her hormones were completely quiescent.

Jake arrived early for the game. The Zamboni was cleaning the ice, and there was no sign of Daniel. He hunched his shoulders inside his leather jacket; for all his fine words, he wasn't looking forward to seeing Shaine in Cameron's company for the next two hours. More fodder for the gossip mill, he thought dryly.

Did Daniel like Cameron?

Then his heart jolted in his chest as Shaine walked in the door with Daniel, who then disappeared into the dressing room. Shaine saw Jake, hesitated fractionally and walked toward him. She was wearing tailored wool slacks with a heavy-knit sweater patterned in rust and green, shiny leather boots on her feet. He could have made love with her on the ice. "Where's Cameron?" he asked.

"He had to phone his mother. He'll be here shortly."

"Are you going to sleep with him tonight?"

He hadn't meant to ask that. "I thought I'd have an orgy with my son as chaperone," she said sweetly.

"It's ludicrous," Jake said with an undertone of savagery, "there's a total lack of basic chemistry between you and Cameron and I still can't stand the thought of him staying overnight in your house."

"You're jealous!" she said incredulously.

"Darn right I am."

Laughter tilted her mouth. "Not half as jealous as I was of Kimberly-Anne Standish when you dated her in grade twelve. She was blond and stacked, while I was thirteen years old with a flat chest and a mop of red hair."

"I never even kissed Kimberly-Anne. She only liked me because I was a hockey star." He added hopefully, "Were you jealous of Marilee, the woman in the magazine article?"

"Of course not!"

"I never kissed her, either. She was much too interested in spending my money."

"Oh," said Shaine. Her lips firmed. "Leave Cameron alone—he's been a good friend to me. He's taken me to galleries in Toronto, loaned me expensive art books that I couldn't afford to buy, and he's sold my work across the country."

"He's also fallen in love with you."

"I've done nothing to encourage him."

He believed her. Going on the offensive, Jake said, "I was looking at Daniel's skates the last time I was here. He should have better ones."

Her head snapped up. "I can't afford better ones."

"But I can. I'll write down his size before I leave."

One of Shaine's greatest fears was that Jake might buy his way into her son's affections. "He's happy with the skates he has."

"He'll be happier with the ones I buy him. Maybe I'll invite him to New York and we'll buy them together."

"He wouldn't go."

"If you came with him, he would." Jake added ruthlessly, "Cameron took you to Toronto and loaned you books. But I can take you to Barcelona and Prague and Bangkok. I'll show you tropical rainforests, Pacific atolls, the Great Barrier Reef...cactus blooming in the desert, monarch butterflies in Mexico...all the colors you're craving to experience firsthand."

"Don't," she whispered. "Don't be cruel, Jake—you know I can't go with you, don't torment me like that. Oh no, here comes Cameron."

Jake said flatly, "We're not done with this, Shaine." Simmering with the force of his emotions, he went to sit on the bleachers. He shouldn't have come on so strong. But Doc was right: somehow he had to get Shaine and Daniel out of Cranberry Cove.

What happened after that was anyone's guess.

The surface of the ice gleamed like the glass Shaine worked with. The teams came out for a warm-up and the game began. He could see Shaine cheering and yelling her support; Cameron in his navy blazer was doing his best not to look bored. Daniel was playing with reckless disregard for his own safety, but always as the member of a team.

Maybe Shaine was right, and Daniel did belong here. Maybe it would be unkind to enlarge the boy's horizons and make him dissatisfied with his own life. For Jake to take risks on the stock market was one thing; but to risk his son's happiness quite another.

When had he ever been so racked with self-doubt?

The first period ended in a tie. Jake chatted with some of his former neighbors, skillfully fending off questions he didn't want to answer. Halfway through the second period, the score was still tied. Then, in a fierce scrimmage for the puck behind the net, Daniel got wedged into the boards and thrown to the ice with bruising force. He lay still, his body in a tight curl of pain.

Jake's blood stopped in his veins. Gripped by a terror unlike any he'd ever known, he surged to his feet, leaped down the bleachers and over the boards. Kneeling beside his son, he said urgently, "Daniel—are you okay?"

The referee said, "He's just winded—had the breath knocked out of him. He'll be fine in a minute."

"Are you sure?" Jake said hoarsely.

"Seen it often enough. Come on, Jake, you've been there."

It was utterly different when it was his own son. Then Daniel took a long, painful breath. His eyes opened. Dimly aware that Shaine was kneeling beside him on the ice, Jake watched the boy resurface to awareness. Daniel looked right up at him and said weakly, "Leave me alone. I don't need you."

Feeling as though he'd been stabbed in the gut, Jake pushed himself to his feet. His leather soles skidded on the ice as he made his way to the gate and the concrete floor. He was bleeding to death inside, he thought distantly, and there was no cure. From a long way away, he saw Daniel being helped onto the bench and replaced with another player. The game resumed.

Shaine plunked herself down beside Jake. He wasn't a man to flaunt his feelings; the sick agony in his eyes made her want to weep. Resting her hand on his sleeve, not caring how many of the villagers were watching, she said forcibly, "He'll come around, Jake, I know he will. You've just got to give him time."

She was mouthing clichés when all he wanted to do was leave by the nearest door. Go back to New York and lick his wounds.

Just as he had thirteen years ago? Hadn't he learned anything? "You're wrong, but thanks for trying to help," he said heavily. "You'd better go back to Cameron."

"Daniel tolerates Cameron. They haven't got a single thing in common. Not like you and Daniel."

He glanced over at her. Meeting his gaze squarely, she said, "Why don't you ask Daniel if he'd go to New York with you? Sooner or later he has to see where and how you live."

The generosity of her offer, its sheer unexpectedness, took Jake aback. Feeling as though the breath had been knocked from his own lungs, he said, "But you're afraid he'll fall for my money and all it can buy. He's only twelve...you could scarcely blame him for being susceptible."

"I have to trust him, don't I? Trust the values I've done my best to instill in him." She paused. "And I have to trust you, as well."

Touched in a place he'd kept closely guarded for years, Jake said in a low voice, "No wonder I always liked you so much. You're so goddamned brave, Shaine. So honest."

"I'm not always honest and I'm scared out of my wits," she said flatly. "But you've come back to the cove and we've got to deal with it—change is the one thing I can't stop."

He was scared, too. Scared Daniel would say no to a trip to New York. Scared to ask Shaine what she meant by honesty? "I'll try and catch up with him in the next couple of days."

Wanting to take the haunted look from Jake's face, Shaine said lightly, "At least with Cameron here, no one has asked me when you and I are getting married."

"You'll have to come up with a new reply. Now that you've turned me down."

She gave an inelegant snort, getting to her feet. "If I'd said yes, you'd be halfway around the globe by now."

"Try me."

Her lashes dropped. "There's courage and there's insanity. Don't push your luck—Cameron might start to look pretty good in comparison."

"You terrify me," Jake said, and grinned at her retreating back. Feeling minimally better, he watched the rest of the game, dropped into Tom and Gertrude's for tea and crowberry muffins and drove back to the motel. Where, once again, he dreamed about Shaine.

Jake didn't return to the cove until he was sure Cameron was well on his way to Toronto. At seven that evening, he crossed the grass toward Shaine's back door. If Daniel was home, he'd offer the boy a visit to New York. What else was he to do? It was up to him to make the first move.

The sun was sliding toward the sea, the kitchen windows open to the cool golden air. As he walked closer, he heard voices from inside. "We have to talk about it sometime, Daniel," Shaine was saying. "Jake's not going to go away just because you want him to."

Jake froze in his tracks as Daniel retorted, "You said he'd only stay a week. It's nearly up."

"But he'll be back. I'm almost sure of that."

Almost, thought Jake. So she didn't entirely trust him. He held himself very still, his shadow elongated on the neatly clipped grass. He shouldn't be listening; his mother would be horrified.

"I wouldn't bet on it," Daniel said.

"Jake's your father. Sooner or later you have to accept that. I know he's late on the scene—but that's partly my fault."

"He went away and left you!"

Jake grimaced. Shaine said steadily, "Yes, he did. But he didn't know I was pregnant. When I found out, I should have tried to trace him. To at least tell him, and give him the choice of what he wanted to do. But I didn't even try.

Not then, and not later when he was becoming so well known it would have been simple to track him down. I was too angry and too hurt, I guess, to bother.'' She sighed. ''But I should have. I've robbed both of you by being so stubborn.''

Some of the tension relaxed in Jake's jaw; he had to admire how straightforwardly she'd admitted to that long-ago mistake.

There was a long silence, which Shaine broke by saying vehemently, ''It's not as though Jake knew about you and stayed away—that would be unforgivable.''

''Yeah, Mum, I get it.''

Jake heard a chair scrape and the tap running. Then Daniel said edgily, ''You gonna marry Cameron?''

''Absolutely not.''

''He doesn't know the blue line from center ice.''

''He knows about a lot of other things,'' Shaine said firmly.

''You gonna marry my father, then?''

''You're the sixth person to ask me that since yesterday!''

''The kids at school are laying bets.''

''Oh, Daniel, I'm sorry…we live in a fishbowl in this damn place, you can't break your fingernail without someone finding out about it.''

''You're not supposed to swear, Mum,'' Daniel said smugly.

''I can't marry Jake just because he's turned up out of the blue,'' Shaine said in exasperation. ''Thirteen years have gone by—I'm a different woman. I was only eighteen when he left and now I'm thirty-one.''

''Pretty old,'' her son said.

''Oh, hush. Anyway, your home is here, Jake travels all over the world, and he and I don't love each other. It's impossible. Talking of home, you've got homework.''

''Gee, thanks for reminding me.''

Shaine's voice softened. "I love you—that hasn't changed."

"Me, too," Daniel mumbled, and thudded his way up the stairs.

He and I don't love each other... The last person Jake wanted to see right now was Shaine. He backtracked, keeping behind the garage, and hurried to his car. Then he drove to the motel, watched a very noisy war movie on video and went to bed.

Jake woke early the next morning. After switching on his laptop, he immersed himself in work for the better part of the day. Then he did a few Internet searches and drove into Cranberry Cove. He'd timed it right. School was out and Daniel was clumping along the road. His T-shirt advertised a local brand of beer; his wide-legged jeans sagged around his hips. Jake pulled over and rolled down the window. "Let me drive you home," he suggested.

Daniel hitched at his waistband. "Okay."

As Jake pulled into Shaine's driveway, he said, "Hold on a minute, Daniel, there's something I want to ask you." He half turned in the seat so he was facing the boy. "You've got a couple of days off after midterms and then it's the long weekend...I'd like you and your mother to come away with me for a few days. We'd go to the Canary Islands first, there's some interesting stained glass there your mother would like; and you could swim and windsurf. Then we'd come back via New York—I have a season's pass for the NHL games, plus I could get you into a practice session with one of the best amateur teams in the state. I'd like to buy you some new skates, too—top of the line."

Daniel had been staring at him, his jaws agape. But at the mention of new skates, the boy's eyes flicked Jake's skin like a knife. "My skates are fine. Mum did without new boots so I could have those skates."

Jake banged on the wheel with the flat of his hand. "I'm

doing this all wrong. I'm not trying to bribe you with a pair of skates, and I don't want to be throwing my money in your face. But there's no use hiding the facts—I do have a lot more money than anyone in Cranberry Cove.'' He took the plunge. ''I just want you to see where I live. How I live. Then maybe you'd come down on your own some time later on, and stay with me.''

''So if Mum came along, we could go to an NHL game?'' As Jake nodded, Daniel smiled almost shyly, a smile that lit up his face. Then he said longingly, ''I've never windsurfed.''

''I could teach you the basics. You're strong and you've got good balance, you'd catch on fast.''

''I learned how to ski pretty quick.''

''Then windsurfing would be a piece of cake.''

''Did my mum say she'd go?''

''I haven't asked her yet. Thought I should check with you first.''

''She's at the shop today.''

''So you'd go, Daniel?''

''The Canary Islands are near Africa—all that way to see some stained glass?''

It didn't seem the time for Jake to mention his private jet. ''I want your mother to enjoy the trip, as well.''

''If she'd go, I would,'' Daniel said in a rush, and for a moment a scared little boy looked out of his eyes.

Unbearably touched, Jake said, ''Why don't you tell her about it? Then I'll come by after supper and check it out with her.'' He wanted Shaine to have time to think about it; he was almost certain if he asked her now, she'd say no. ''I'll see you later, Daniel.''

After the boy got out of the car, Jake drove off; he'd been invited for dinner with Emily Bennett. For dessert Emily served a bakeapple cheesecake decorated with whipped cream. Jake sat back afterward, testing his belt.

"I'll have to jog an extra five miles tomorrow." He grinned. "But it was worth it, Emily. That was wonderful."

They washed the dishes, chatting easily; then Jake said, "I'm on my way to see Shaine. I'm hoping I can persuade her and Daniel to go on a short holiday with me."

"Don't you play with her affections now, Jake," Emily said sternly.

"She won't let me."

"Then I wish you the best of luck."

Jake was remembering this as he tapped on Shaine's door. She pulled it open, her cheeks flushed with temper. "You'd better come in," she said, "so we can fight without the whole street hearing."

It was a fight she wasn't going to win, he thought, as he followed her into the kitchen. "Where's Daniel?"

"Out with friends. We've got half an hour. The answer's no, I'm not going away with you. This trip is about Daniel and you. Father and son bonding, and all that good stuff. It's nothing to do with me."

"What did Daniel say to that?"

She glared at him. "Oh, you'd done a fine job—he wants me to go. What did you think, that you could coerce me with a stained-glass window?"

"Actually it's a whole roof," he said mildly. "By Pere Valldepérez from Barcelona."

In spite of herself, she felt a desperate tug of longing. "I've heard about him."

"Now's your chance to see one of his most spectacular works," Jake drawled. "And on the same day go swimming in water a lot warmer than what's outside the window."

"I've got a business to run."

"Delegate."

"Daniel would miss some school."

"On the Canaries, he'd be having history and geography lessons he'd never forget."

"I won't get into bed with you!"

"Okay," Jake said casually.

"Not that you look the slightest bit interested."

Her flare-up of temper delighted him. "I'm interested. But you're right, we've got to focus on Daniel." He advanced on her, amused to see her fingers tense on the counter. "Just to keep the record straight, Daniel doesn't want new skates, he told me how you'd done without boots to pay for the ones he's got. So I can't buy my way into his affections." His voice deepened. "You've done a great job bringing him up."

"Thank you," she said in a stifled voice. "This kitchen is plenty big—you don't have to back me into the wall."

"Flustered, Shaine?" he said, running a finger lightly over her lips.

"You are, based on my limited sampling of the population, the sexiest man I've ever met. How am I going to keep that hidden from my son for a whole week and a half?"

"You're a clever woman, you'll think of something."

"You must promise to play fair!"

"You'll go?"

"Only if you swear in blood to treat me as if Maggie Stearns was watching every move."

He laughed. "Your hormones really are in an uproar."

"Yours seem to be fast asleep."

Moving fast, Jake trapped her against the counter, running his hands down her ribs to her waist, then pulling her hips into his as he kissed her hard on the mouth. Desire slamming through him, he backed off fast and gave her a lazy grin. "Just say the word and I'm all attention."

"You're treating this like a joke," she said in a choked voice.

Relenting, he said, "I won't do anything on this trip to cause you embarrassment or distress, I promise. Come on,

Shaine, I'd like you to have a good time. How long since you've had a proper holiday?''

She raised her brows. "Devlin, Padric, Connor and Daniel could empty the refrigerator in one meal. Not to mention things like dentists, hockey gear, school trips and the mortgage on the shop. A long time.''

The Ferrari alone would have paid for all that. Trying to hold guilt at bay, Jake said, "I'll keep this trip low-key. We won't go near my place at the Hamptons, and the Canaries aren't top-end luxury by any means. I don't want to shove my money in your face.''

"You'd have to pay for both of us. I can't afford a trip like that.''

"It would be my privilege," Jake said with raw truth.

And Shaine, once again, found herself melting like wax to the flame. She muttered, "You've just made me agree to something I shouldn't be doing.''

"Good," said Jake. "Tell Daniel the trip's on. I'm heading back to New York early tomorrow, and I'll call you as soon as I have the dates finalized—give me a couple of days. I'll meet you at the airport in Deer Lake, how would that be?''

He sounded very business-like, he thought in exasperation. Was that so she wouldn't guess how ridiculously happy he felt? Happy because Daniel had agreed to spend some time with him, of course. But for eight or nine days he'd be with Shaine. Giving her the gift of a holiday. Not diamonds or orchids or a shopping spree in Paris; just a break from the hard routine of years.

Giving something back to the woman who'd given so much to their son.

It felt wonderful. Money could, on occasion, buy happiness, Jake decided, kissed her lightly on the cheek and left.

Shaine moved to the window where she could see him stride down the path. Change could be exciting. It could also be very frightening. Two of the ways she'd managed to handle the last thirteen years were by not looking any further than the width of the cove; and by keeping to a routine that gave her some control over her life.

Now Jake was changing all that. What if this trip unsettled her so that the constrictions around her became unbearable? It was fine for Jake, he could just return to an existence she could scarcely imagine. But she'd have to come back to the cove. To hockey games and Maggie Stearns and making red and white lighthouses for the tourists.

She sank down at the kitchen table, resting her head in her hands. Jake was like a force of nature, forceful and unstoppable. She wasn't in love with him. Despite what she'd told him, she had been once, and had paid dearly for her mistake: so dearly that she now wouldn't admit that long-ago love to him. But his muscular, rangy body still fascinated her, as did his rapier intelligence and the unconscious aura of power he wore as easily as his faded jeans.

Which, to be honest, she wanted to rip from his body.

Shaine groaned. She didn't think he'd disappear again, not now that he'd met Daniel. She'd come to trust his commitment to his son that day at the rink when Daniel had been thrown against the boards. But once this trip was over, he wouldn't need her anymore. He could invite Daniel on his own to New York and Switzerland and all the other places she longed to go.

She'd be the outsider.

Alone, as she'd been all too often in the village where she'd grown up. Alone and celibate, she thought with an unhappy droop to her lips.

But how could she wish Jake had never come back? For Daniel's sake, she couldn't possibly do that.

She was trapped. Tasting freedom but unable to choose it. Being with Jake but unable to make love with him.

She was glad he couldn't see her now.

CHAPTER NINE

THE skylight soared above Shaine, great pyramids of glass in a stark metal framework. Enraptured, she stared upward, losing herself in a shimmer of gold, red and orange accented by triangles of clear glass.

Jake said to Daniel, "Let's wander around, she'll be here for a while."

They'd flown from Tenerife that morning to the smaller island of Gran Canaria, then driven north to the harbor city of Las Palmas de Gran Canaria. The skylight was in a magnificent stone auditorium designed for classical music; in the last few years, Jake had attended more than one baroque concert in the main hall with its sweeping view of the sea.

Someone was practicing in one of the smaller rooms. Jake listened with pleasure to the sonorous notes of a cello, then said easily, "You might as well know the worst about me, Daniel. I go for that kind of music."

"No kidding?"

"Always have. Got me into a few fights at school."

"Kinda weird," Daniel said, his head cocked as a violin and piano joined in.

"It ain't rap."

Daniel gave a bark of laughter. His wariness had begun to diminish yesterday, when he'd had his first windsurfing lesson. He'd gotten drenched, dumped and tossed by waves; but he'd persevered, and Jake would long remember the sheer delight on his son's face as his sail had caught the wind and he'd scudded across the water for all of sixty seconds.

They wandered outside, found an ice-cream vendor and sat under a palm tree to eat their cones. When they went

back in to find Shaine, she was just closing her sketch book.
"Wonderful," she breathed. "Thanks so much for bringing
me here, Jake."

"No problem. We could go shopping for a while, have
lunch and go south to the beach before we head back to
Tenerife."

"That sounds like a great way to spend a day," Shaine
said with a contented sigh. In a flowered sundress that bared
her shoulders and a lot of leg, she looked relaxed and
happy; Jake wanted to kiss her so badly that he glanced
away, scared his feelings showed on his face. He'd been
doing his best to treat both his son and Shaine with a casual
friendliness that was open to any overtures, but that made
no claims on them. He wasn't finding this easy. But he was
determined to stick with it. Low-key was his motto for this
holiday; although even as he repeated the words in his
mind, he remembered Daniel's awed face as he checked
out the amenities on Jake's private jet.

As they wandered Calle Mayor de Triana with its styl-
ishly ornamented stone facades, Shaine found a display
case of very elegant sunglasses, and stopped to choose a
pair. Daniel tugged at Jake's sleeve. "I want to get her a
present," he whispered, "but I can't afford anything here."

"We'll go to a market on Tenerife. You'll find something there. Getting hungry?"

Daniel, so he'd discovered, was always hungry. They
found a restaurant whose patio was shaded by Canary
palms and tall poinsettia shrubs splashed with red, where
they ate watercress soup, delicious prawns and balls of *go-
fio* dipped in a fiery sauce called *mojo*. Daniel and Shaine
both had flambéed bananas, Daniel following that with an
avocado milk shake. "Let's go to the beach," he said.

"I need a siesta," Shaine moaned, "it's a custom I could
get used to," and gave Jake a comical grimace as Daniel
hauled her to her feet.

Playa del Ingles was crowded and noisy. Jake rented a

windsurfer for Daniel, then plunged into the waves with Shaine. She'd bought herself a minimalist bikini at their hotel in Tenerife, because the swimsuit she'd brought from home had seemed far too staid. She still felt shy wearing the scraps of turquoise fabric; and knew she'd never have the nerve to go topless like some of the young women sauntering along the beach. Daniel, she could tell, was doing his embarrassed best to ignore them. Jake, with the impeccable good manners that were beginning to grate on her, had never mentioned them.

She'd been the one to insist this would be a platonic holiday. So why was she complaining that for the last two days Jake could have been one of her brothers?

She lay down on her towel so she could watch Daniel struggling with his sail. Jake glanced over at her. Sun glazed the salt water on her skin, her spine was a long, luscious curve, and her cleavage in her brief bikini top was calculated to drive him haywire. He said pleasantly, "I'll go rent a board and stay with Daniel for a while—will you be all right on your own?"

"I'll be fine," she said brightly, and watched him walk away from her, a tall, narrow-hipped man whose muscles rippled under his tanned skin. She buried her face in her towel with a muffled groan. She wasn't going to let a case of out-of-control lust ruin a marvelous holiday.

When she looked up, Jake had joined Daniel in the waves. As Jake lifted the sail on his own board, obviously demonstrating something to his son, Shaine saw how closely Daniel was paying attention. Then the two of them waded further into the water. It hurt something deep inside her to see them together. But why should it hurt? She should be happy.

After this amazing holiday, how was she ever going to settle down in Cranberry Cove?

*   *   *

The next morning, back on Tenerife, Jake realized a family had moved into the bungalow next to theirs: father, mother and a son about the same age as Daniel. The bungalows, whitewashed with tile roofs, were separated by palm trees and tall trellises draped with bougainvillea; but a pathway to one of the outdoor restaurants linked them. On their way to breakfast, the other parents smiled at Shaine, Jake and Daniel; the two boys eyed each other warily. "We just arrived last night," the man said. "Where would you recommend we have breakfast? I'm Ben Latimer, by the way. My wife, Andrea, and my son, Jasper."

"Jake Reilly, Shaine and Daniel," Jake responded, neatly avoiding any mention of the word wife. "Why don't you come along with us? The pavilion overlooking the ocean pool serves incredible fruit and omelettes."

Andrea smiled at Shaine; she was a pretty brunette. "Have you been here long?"

"This is our third day. I love it here."

"Your first time on the Canaries?"

Her first time anywhere, Shaine thought wryly, and began talking about their visit to Gran Canaria. Jake and Ben had moved ahead on the path; behind her, Shaine heard Jasper say, "Can you windsurf at the beach?"

"Yep. It's not too windy, not like at Playa de Médano. I just started a couple days ago."

"Let's go after breakfast. I had three lessons before we came."

"Sure thing."

A companionship sprang up very naturally as they all ate locally grown papaya, bananas and figs, along with delicious pastries. Ben and Andrea seemed to take it for granted that Shaine and Jake were husband and wife; Jake did nothing to disabuse this notion, shrinking from the inevitable explanations. But it gave him an odd feeling when Ben said casually, "Would you and your wife join us at the beach in half an hour? That way the boys can windsurf."

"Sounds good," Jake said. What would it be like if Shaine was his wife?

Shaine in his bed every night...

With the help of Ben and Jake, the two boys progressed from waist-deep in the water to upright on their boards with the sails catching the wind; after the first capsize, any barriers between them were gone. Shaine said to Andrea, "I'm glad Daniel and Jasper are getting along so well. Daniel's having a great time."

As they began filling in each other's backgrounds, Shaine managed to imply that Jake spent at least half his time in Newfoundland, traveling from there to look after his business interests. Andrea had taken a course in stained glass, so her questions were both genuinely interested and intelligent; she herself was a teacher.

The day drifted by, with a trip into Los Cristianos and a stroll along the crowded promenade that afternoon. The next day all six of them drove through forests of laurel and pine toward Pico del Teide, the high, cloud-draped volcanic peak in the center of the island. Shaine was entranced by the enormous craters of the Cañadas, yellow, red and gray, and by a landscape that was a desert of iridescent black lava. After she'd taken innumerable pictures and made a series of rapid sketches in her book, she said, "I can't wait to get back in my studio! Jake, this is so exciting."

Most of the women he'd dated had affected an air of having seen everything that was worth seeing and of not being overly impressed by any of it. But Shaine was different; Shaine felt passionately about life in all its rich and varied hues. Briefly he rested his palm on her cheek. "You're sweet," he said, "I like you," and found he didn't give a damn if Ben, Andrea, Jasper and Daniel heard every word he was saying.

Her eyes huge, her cheeks delicately flushed in a way that had nothing to do with the heat, she whispered, "This trip—I've never had a gift like it."

Would she grow accustomed to his wealth, he wondered, take it for granted in the way those other women had? Somehow he didn't think so. Shaine was too rooted in Cranberry Cove for that to happen. "To see you so happy," he said, "it makes me feel...I don't even know how it makes me feel."

"Come on, Jake, say it—you're happy, too."

He was. Standing in a bleak moonscape in the brutal heat, he wouldn't have traded places with anyone in the world.

Her smile brilliant, she added, "We'd better catch up with the others."

"The Latimers are taking some of the pressure off, aren't they?" he said slowly. "Daniel isn't thrown so much on my company in a way that might not have worked. And they're three more reasons for me to keep my hands off you."

Daniel and Jasper were seeing who could throw rocks the furthest into the giant crater, watched indulgently by Ben and Andrea, who were holding hands. "I already have three brothers," Shaine said roundly. "I don't need a fourth."

"What do you need, Shaine?"

Under the broad brim of her straw hat, her cheeks were now the scarlet of poinsettias. "That would be telling," she said, pivoted and hurried across the uneven ground toward the others.

Grinning to himself, Jake followed. In the next few days they swam, lazed on the beach, ate fish fresh from the Atlantic, visited a vineyard and wandered around some of the picturesque little towns of the north coast. Goats, orange trees, ornately carved wooden verandas, white candleberry blooming against the walls of square-towered churches: Shaine admired and photographed them all. They had a farewell dinner with the Latimers on their last night. Shaine drank rather a lot of wine and danced with Jake in a way that wasn't entirely discreet; her son, he was pleased to note as he tried to ease away from her body, was absorbed in a game of chess with Jasper.

Before the month was out, he was going to take Shaine to bed.

But not tonight.

This resolve was sorely tested when the three of them went back to the bungalow. On the balcony, which was laced with vines and filled with the soft murmur of the sea, Shaine threw her arms around his neck. "I've had so much fun the last few days!"

Daniel was looking at them both askance. Jake stepped back and said with real sincerity, "I'm glad." Then he kissed her with brotherly propriety on the cheek and said good night.

They left Aeropuerto de Gando early the next morning. All three of them slept through the transatlantic crossing; a limo met them at Kennedy International Airport, inching through the traffic toward Jake's condo, which overlooked the trees and pathways of Central Park. His spacious, high-ceilinged rooms, with their priceless carpets and few, well-chosen artworks weren't Shaine's idea of low-key, an opinion she kept to herself.

Pizza and a movie that night, visits to all the standard tourist attractions the next day, and then it was their final day in the city. Daniel and Jake left midmorning for his hockey practice; Shaine stayed behind, wanting to do some shopping. She had two things in mind. The first was easy, involving picking up a package that she'd arranged for the day before. But the second took some serious thought. The first three shops she went into had prices that were through the roof; she got out, fast. But the fourth, a smaller boutique, was just within her range. The saleswoman was middle-aged and intimidatingly elegant. "Can I help you, madam?"

Go for it, thought Shaine. After all, you'll never see the woman again. She said clearly, "I want a nightgown that will make a man who's treating me like I'm his sister do otherwise."

The woman glanced from Shaine's vibrant cap of hair to her lightly tanned features in which her eyes were set like gems. Then they skimmed her slender figure with professional expertise. "That man's a dolt and let me see what I can do," she said pleasantly.

"I wish I could say the sky's the limit as far as price is concerned—but I can't," Shaine gulped, blurting out a sum she couldn't exceed; even that meant she'd be eating frugally for a month. "And he's not really a dolt...it's complicated."

"It always is," the woman said dryly, and selected four nightgowns from the rack. "Why don't you try these while I look for more?"

Nightgowns that bared, that revealed, that hinted, that clung: Shaine tried them all. In the end she decided on an ecru satin gown that skimmed her hips and breasts, softly shadowing her cleavage. The power of suggestion, she'd always thought, was more powerful than outright nakedness; and if this didn't make Jake forget he was behaving like Devlin, nothing would.

She wanted, just once, to break her self-imposed celibacy. She'd visited Doc a while ago, so she was protected against another pregnancy; and maybe going to bed with Jake would break the hold he had over her. Set her free in a way she hadn't been for thirteen long years. It was worth a try.

The saleswoman wrapped the gown exquisitely in tissue

and a beribboned bag. Shaine thanked her warmly, hurried back to the condo and hid the bag before the others got back. But the other package she put on the bookshelf.

When Daniel walked in the door, he was soaked in sweat and incandescent with excitement. "Mum, you shoulda seen the coach, he was so cool. He taught me a whole new way to feint in front of the net, and the other guys on the team were neat, too—we practiced passing for over half an hour. The coach said if I was down this way again, I could go to another practice, he said I was a good player. A real good player is what he said." Daniel gave his mother a dazzled smile. "Is there any Pepsi in the refrigerator?" Then he looked down at himself, dumping his bag on the polished parquet floor. "Man, do I need a shower."

Jake said easily, "One Pepsi so you don't spoil your lunch. We'll eat in half an hour, okay?"

"Yeah, sure." Daniel looked right at Jake, his blue eyes still vivid with excitement. "Thanks," he said, "that was awesome."

"Any time," Jake said, his throat tight. It would be the icing on the cake were Daniel to call him Dad. But maybe one day he would. It didn't, at the moment, seem impossible.

Daniel swilled the Pepsi and ran toward the bathroom, slicing at the floor with an imaginary hockey stick. The door slammed shut behind him. Shaine winced. "Does an adolescent male ever walk anywhere?"

"You've brought up four of 'em—you should know."

"It was a rhetorical question." Then she got up and picked up the package on the bookshelf. "I have something for you," she said awkwardly. "I can't thank you enough for everything you've done, Jake. But I thought this might make a start."

Jake took the small, flat package, which she'd wrapped in bright red foil, and turned it over in his hands. When had a woman last given him a gift? Ever since he'd made his first million, he'd been the one expected to do the giving. He said, "You don't know how often this last week I thought of buying you something. Now I wish I had. But I didn't want to make you feel indebted."

"You've given us both so much," Shaine said with a sweet smile. "More than we can ever repay."

He was a man known for thinking fast on his feet and outwitting world-renowned financial experts; but right now he was fumbling for words. "I've had fun this week. Simple, ordinary fun, the kind you can't buy. That's one of the things I've been in danger of losing the last few years. So it's not all one way, Shaine."

"What else have you lost?"

My heart, he thought crazily. To you. "That's a conversation for a leisurely dinner with lots of wine," he said with a crooked smile. "Should I open my present?"

She nodded, watching as he unpeeled the foil. Inside the box, in a simple pewter frame, was a photograph she'd taken on the beach below their bungalow at Costa Adeje: Jake and Daniel side by side in the waves, laughing at each other, their boards floating alongside. Jake was staring at the photo as though he'd been poleaxed. She said anxiously, "Don't you like it?"

"You couldn't have given me anything better," he said huskily. "How did you get it all together?"

"I had the photos developed while we were at the resort, and the framing done here."

She'd taken time and trouble, in other words. His chest congested with an emotion he couldn't have named, he took her face in his hands and kissed her as if she was the only woman in the world. Her response was immediate and generous. Then he heard the bathroom door open and Daniel start down the hall toward them, his bare feet squeaking on the parquet. With a reluctance he didn't bother hiding, Jake released Shaine. "Has Daniel seen this?"

She shook her head. As the boy came into the living room, Jake said, "Your mother had this photo framed for me. I'll treasure it, Daniel."

Daniel looked at the photograph, then up at the man holding it. "We go back home tomorrow," he said in an unreadable voice.

"I hope you'll come to New York again, though. Perhaps over Christmas."

"I got a hockey tournament."

"If we want to see each other," Jake said carefully, "we can always figure something out."

Daniel blurted, "I got you a present in Tenerife. And one for Mum."

He took off down the hall, his hair still wet from the shower. When he came back, he thrust one paper bag at Shaine, the other at Jake. Shaine's gift was a beautiful white cotton placemat edged with handmade Vilaflor lace. "I could only afford one," Daniel said. "I thought it would look nice on the table by the TV."

Touched, she said, "It's beautiful, Daniel…lace-making is another old craft that hasn't died out, rather like stained glass."

When Jake opened his bag, he saw a small wooden carving of a windsurfer, the man's back braced, the sail a smooth curve. He couldn't choke up twice in ten minutes, he thought. "Perfect," he said, and took the risk he'd been wanting to take all week: he put his arms around his son and gave him a quick, hard hug. Before Daniel could react either way, Jake stepped back. Picking up the carving, he put it on the bookshelf beside a priceless Donatello bronze; and knew which one he valued more highly.

Clearing his throat, he said, "Natural history museum

this afternoon, dinner at a bistro down the street, then we'll go to the hockey game.''

His condo was going to be distressingly empty when they were gone. And knew, the next evening, that his forecast had been all too accurate. He'd put Shaine and Daniel on his jet bound for Deer Lake, gone to meetings all day, and now he was sitting in a leather chair by his bookshelf, looking at a photo and a simple wood carving and knowing he was in deep trouble.

CHAPTER TEN

AT MIDNIGHT the following Sunday, Shaine was washing dishes in her kitchen. Her brothers had just left. In company with Daniel, she'd shown them most of the photos she'd taken on their holiday. A few she'd kept back: snapshots of Jake that she'd taken on impulse. When she'd gotten all the photos back from the shop, she'd been shocked to discover just how many such impulses she'd succumbed to.

She didn't have to show anyone else those photos; some things were meant to be kept private.

Like the nightgown she'd bought in New York. She and Jake had yet to make love; the nightgown was still neatly folded in tissue paper and stored on the top shelf of her closet.

Would she ever get to wear it?

She felt horribly wide awake. Jake had called two days ago, spoken to her briefly and then talked to Daniel for several minutes. She wanted Jake to take his fatherly responsibilities seriously. So why had that phone call left her as restless as the waves on the sea?

Cranberry Cove seemed even more constrictive than usual; and celibacy a cold choice. What was she going to do? Settle back into her life as though that holiday had never happened? Or take charge of change and shape it to suit herself?

On Monday morning Jake was packing for a four-day business trip to Chicago and California when the phone rang. "Jake Reilly," he barked into the receiver.

"It's Shaine."

His voice warmed. "How are you? And how's Daniel?"

"We're both fine."

The pause went on too long. "You're sure you're okay?" he said sharply.

"Are you free next weekend?"

"Yes," he said, without even checking his date book.

"I'm going away on Thursday for my annual buying trip—there's a wonderful glass shop in Old Montreal. If you wanted to join me, I—"

"I'll join you," he said promptly.

Her voice high-pitched, she said, "I want to go to bed with you. That's why I'm phoning."

"You're on."

"I—what did you say?"

Jake said patiently, "Yes, I'd be delighted to meet you in Montreal, and yes, I'd like to go to bed with you."

Like? Desperate would be a more accurate word.

"Oh," said Shaine. "Really?"

"I might have been acting like one of your brothers in the Canaries, but my thoughts were far from fraternal. That green bikini falls into the category of cruel and unusual punishment."

"It's turquoise and you hardly gave me a second glance!"

"That's what you think," Jake said, deciding he sounded remarkably childish and not caring one whit. "I was endeavoring to protect our son from the sordid facts of life. Who'll look after him on the weekend?"

"Devlin." Unmistakable panic in her tone, she added, "Daniel mustn't find out about us meeting in Montreal—it's between you and me."

"Of course," he said soothingly. "I know a wonderful old inn in Vieux-Montréal, I'll make a reservation. When do you arrive?"

"I can't afford—"

"I can."

With more of her usual spirit, she sniffed, "You'd better watch out. I could get accustomed to high-class living."

She had yet to experience anything Jake would have called high-class. "You let me worry about that," he said. "When do you get there?"

"Thursday evening. I spend most of Friday at the glass shop. I'd have to fly home Sunday morning."

He did some rapid mental shuffling. "I can meet you at the inn late Friday afternoon. Are you home now? I'll call you back in ten minutes."

Quickly, before she could change her mind, he put down the receiver. Shaine wanted to go to bed with him. For thirty-six hours he'd have her to himself. No gossipy neighbors, no brothers, no son. Just himself and Shaine and a shared bed.

His mouth stretched in a broad smile, Jake looked up a number on his Palm Pilot, dialed and switched effortlessly to French. Four minutes later the phone was ringing in Shaine's kitchen. "Hello?" she said breathlessly.

"All set." He gave her the address and room number, and told her they'd be expecting her on Thursday. "Your meals are included, they have two restaurants that are both excellent."

"I'm not doing this because I want another holiday in a fancy hotel," she said with a touch of desperation. "I'm not using you, Jake—that's not what it's about."

"For Pete's sake, Shaine, I know you better than that," Jake said, and found himself wondering what it was about. Shaine being Shaine, he'd no doubt find out on the weekend. "I've got to go, I'm flying out in a couple of hours. I'll see you Friday in time for dinner…and Shaine—thanks."

Shaine made an indecipherable noise and put down the receiver. She'd done it. Taken control.

Well, sort of. On other trips to Montreal, she'd walked past L'Auberge de Jean-Pierre on her wanderings around the old town, and wistfully wished she could afford even a snack inside. Now, because Jake was rich, she was going to stay there.

A wild weekend. She deserved one, didn't she? What was the harm? She was thirty-one years old and she'd lived responsibly for far too long. One weekend wouldn't hurt.

After all, she wasn't in love with Jake. She was never going to risk falling in love with him again. But he had some kind of hold over her; her series of impulsive snap-shots showed that. If she went to bed with him, she'd get him out of her system.

Yes, that's what would happen, she thought blithely, and with a shiver of anticipation remembered the ecru night-gown she'd bought in New York.

He'd like it. She was as certain of that as she was of the tides in the bay.

At six-thirty on Friday Jake arrived at the inn; he was later than he'd planned, because he'd stopped at the airport to make a phone call to the glass shop before it closed.

He looked around appreciatively. The inn's antiques were the real thing, its carpets, although worn, were gen-uine Aubusson, and the service was impeccable. "Madame is waiting for you in the cocktail lounge," the concierge said. "I'll see that your bags are delivered to your room, *m'sieur.*"

Jake slipped a bill into his hand, and headed for the lounge. A woman in a sliver of black dress was perched on a stool at the counter; her legs in sheer black hose seemed to go on forever. As he walked toward her over the stone floor, her red hair shot fire under the soft lighting. He lifted her hand, pressing his lips into her palm. Her fingers were cold. "Hello, Shaine," he said softly. "Finish your drink and we'll go upstairs. That's what you want, isn't it? I know it's what I want."

She tossed back the last of her red wine and stood up in

a single graceful movement. She was taller than usual. "Nice shoes," he added, admiring the turn of her ankle above slender black stilettos.

She glanced around the mahogany-paneled luxury of their surroundings; no one was in earshot. "From the consignment store," she said.

"Our secret. The dress?"

"I made it. I didn't have to buy much fabric."

Her arms were bare and the dress dipped in the back. His mouth dry, Jake said, "A hundred and one ways to save money?"

"I could write the book. How was California?"

"A million miles away," he said, and watched an enchanting flush spread over her cheeks. With his hand at her back, they left the bar and took the polished brass elevator to the top floor, where he'd reserved the inn's only suite. As she slipped her key into the lock and stepped inside, she said, "The flowers are beautiful, thank you, Jake...I only wish I could take them home with me."

He'd ordered flowers to be there when she arrived, dusky red roses for the living room and a pure white orchid in full bloom for the bedroom. Locking the door behind him, he threw his jacket over the leather couch, tugged his tie off and said, "This time, I've brought protection. Come here, Shaine."

"And I went to see Doc," she announced. She looked as edgy and high-strung as a racehorse about to bolt from the starting gate. "I've done this before with you. I don't know why I'm so nervous."

"It matters, what we do here this weekend—that's why you're nervous."

"It's a wild weekend," she retorted. "Not a trip to the altar."

And if that wasn't a challenge, he didn't know what was. As he kicked off his shoes, Shaine said edgily, "I won't be a minute." She grabbed a ribboned bag from the bureau drawer and disappeared into the bathroom. Jake peeled off his socks and waited.

Then the door opened and Shaine walked toward him. A muscle twitched in his jaw. Her nightgown shimmered and rippled in the light, flowing over her waist and hips, clinging to her thighs. He could see the jut of her nipples, the tilt of her breasts, and felt his groin harden. He said at random, "You didn't buy that in Cranberry Cove."

"New York," she replied, and with a sudden impish grin added, "Do you like it?"

His answer was to pick her up in his arms, cradling her, the fabric slithering seductively against his wrists. Carrying her into the velvet-draped bedroom, he laid her down on the bed. Light from the other room bathed her in gold. Sitting beside her, he stroked first the arch of one foot and then the other.

"Kiss me," she whispered.

"No rush," he said lazily, unbuttoning his shirt and throwing it over a chair. Very gently he eased the nightgown up, smoothing her inner thighs, his hands always moving imperceptibly upward. She moaned his name, her eyes dark pools of desire, her hips seeking out his touch. When he found the juncture of her thighs, he knelt on the bed beside her and touched her with exquisite control until she was writhing beneath his fingers, her sobs of breath like music to his ears. Then she broke, crying out in fierce pleasure as he brought her to fulfillment.

When she could speak, she gasped, "How did that happen? I'm the one who's supposed to be seducing you."

He unbuckled his belt and let his suit trousers slide to the floor. "You are," he said. Catching his mood, she sat up and with sensuous slowness lifted her gown over her head; her skin gleamed like ivory silk and the scent of her perfume drifted to his nostrils. The fragrance of flowers, he thought, colorful and passionate like Shaine herself.

Then she reached for his shoulders and drew him closer

until her breasts were brushing the hard wall of his torso. He said jaggedly, "There's never been a woman as beautiful as you," and dropped his head into the shadowed valley between her breasts.

Unerringly he found their peaks, teasing them with his fingertips; then he cupped each sweet, firm rise in his palms. He could feel the hammering of her heartbeat against his flesh, an intimacy that bound him all the more closely to her; with deliberate leisure he brushed his lips over her nipples until, once again, she was moving frantically against him. "Now," she begged. "Jake, please... now."

Swiftly ridding himself of his underwear, he pushed her back into the pillows, lying on top of her, pressing into the heated, moist readiness between her thighs. Then he swooped to plunder her mouth, heat streaking through his veins.

Deep inside, Shaine felt the tension mount to an unbearable peak. Her whole body shuddering with need, she wrapped her fingers around his silken hardness and with primitive pride watched his face convulse. Lost to everything but the moment, she felt as if all the hues of the rainbow were surrounding her in glorious shafts of color. And it was Jake who had brought her to that place.

She'd never wanted anyone as she wanted him. Never. Whimpering with hunger, she arched her hips to gather him in.

But even then, although his body was screaming for release, Jake held back. Wanting to give her all the pleasure he was capable of, he rubbed himself against her, bringing her powerfully and inexorably to climax.

She said helplessly, her breasts rising and falling with the intensity of her breathing, "You did it again."

"So I did," he said, took her hand and drew it slowly down his body.

"It's my turn now," she said, reached up and kissed him, her tongue plunging to meet his.

Wrapping his arms around her waist, knowing dimly that he was holding the whole world in his embrace, Jake rolled to lie on his side. They were face-to-face, so he could see every change of expression as it flitted across her features. With a candor that charmed him, she said, "I like what we're doing. Your body's so beautiful, Jake. We fit, don't we? Perfectly."

"Of course we do," he said, and nipped her lip between his teeth, his fingers buried in the flame of her hair.

She skimmed his rib cage with tantalizing delicacy, savoring every nuance of bone and muscle. Her nostrils were filled with the scent of his skin, familiar in a way that almost frightened her, wholly masculine. He was male to her female, she thought, her eyes glittering. Her mate.

Gesture followed naturally from gesture, arousal from arousal, as Shaine slid the length of his body, tasting him, teasing him with mouth and hands. Then Jake crushed her in his arms, his breath heated on her bare shoulder. "I can't wait any longer," he rasped. As she clasped his hips and opened to him, welcoming him with all her heart, he drove deep into her body.

Her own breath ravaging her breast, she enclosed him. He could feel her inner throbbing even as he watched the storm gather in her face; and could no longer withstand his own body's torment. Thrusting again and again, he broke within her even as she also broke. His sweat-slicked forehead dropped to her breast; heartbeat mingled with heartbeat, then gradually slowed.

When he thought he could trust his voice, Jake said, "You've finished me off, woman."

She gave a rich, throaty chuckle. "Have I? I'm kind of out of practice."

He was glad to hear it. Fiercely, possessively glad.

Hugging her to his chest, he muttered, "I hate to say this, but I'm hungry. I think I forgot to have lunch."

"I want chocolate éclairs and fresh strawberries," Shaine said. "I already checked the menu."

"Nothing else?"

"Oh, maybe a steak or two."

He felt a wash of such tenderness that for a moment he couldn't breathe. "You can have whatever you want," he said unsteadily.

She threw back her head, her laughter a silvery cascade of sound. "One way or another, I always seem to have fun with you."

Her face was that of a woman who has been well and truly loved. As she sat up, stretching with unconscious grace, her belly concave beneath the wings of her rib cage, he said, "Keep that up and we'll never make it for dinner."

She slid from the bed, her eyes full of mischief. "I'd hate for them to run out of dessert before we get there."

"And we do have all night," Jake said. "We could go dancing after dinner, there's a blues band playing in the lounge. And this time I can hold you as close as I want to."

Standing proud in her nakedness, she whispered, "Then we could come back to bed."

He surged to his feet, pulling her hips into his, his gaze ranging the swollen, seductive softness of her mouth. "I can't get enough of you," he said roughly; and saw with brief unease the way her eyelids dropped to hide her expression.

"I'm sure by Sunday morning you'll have changed your mind," she said, and headed purposely for the bathroom, where she'd left her clothes.

Picking up his trousers, he said, "I don't think so. I may be in this for the long haul, Shaine."

"Jake," she said forcefully, "this is about here and now,

about the two of us enjoying each other. I don't even want to think about tomorrow, let alone a week from now."

She looked very adamant. Another challenge, thought Jake.

If there was one thing he'd learned in the last thirteen years, it was the value, every now and then, of the indirect approach. She was indeed like a high-bred racehorse: not for the faint of heart. He could bide his time. "You just want those chocolate éclairs," he said agreeably, and saw relief flutter over her features.

"A woman of simple tastes, that's me—dynamite sex and whipped cream."

We didn't have sex. We made love.

And where had those words come from? Jake gave her an enigmatic smile before she disappeared into the bathroom to get dressed.

The dining room wouldn't have been out of place in the palace of Versailles. Shaine walked to their table as if she'd been frequenting such elegance all her life; then, as they sat, gave him a wicked grin. "I'm going to enjoy every minute of this," she said, picked up the heavy parchment menu and ran her eyes down the appetizers. "I want one of everything," she said, "how am I ever going to decide?"

"Why don't you start with dessert and work backward?"

"Good idea."

The wild mushroom soup was delicious, the steak tender, the salad crisp and tangy, and the éclairs a deadly combination of smooth chocolate, fluffy cream and flaky crust. Shaine ran her tongue over her lips and sat back with a sigh. "Luscious," she said. "If I had room, I'd start all over again."

She'd missed a tiny blob of cream at the corner of her mouth: her luscious, to use her word, and infinitely kissable mouth. Jake stared at the cream. He was in love with her, he thought, stunned. In love with Shaine. Of course he was, it had been staring him in the face ever since she'd fainted in his arms in her shop.

His mind made another leap. He'd never stopped loving her. That was why he'd not once been tempted to live with another woman, let alone marry her. All along, Shaine had been the woman in his life, the only one who was his match. His soul mate.

She said pertly, "What's the matter? Have I got chocolate on my chin?"

He stared at her as if he'd never seen her before. He wanted to marry her. Live with her day by day, share decisions, joy and sorrow, laughter and tears. Be a father to Daniel. And, perhaps, to another child, this one the fruit of a committed love.

The words were out before he could stop them. "Have you ever thought about having another baby?"

She blinked, her fingers tightening around her fork. "As a single mother? Nope."

"What if you were married?"

"I'm not going to marry. End of discussion. Do you think if I had coffee, I'd be awake all night?"

She didn't have a clue what was going on inside him. Nor, if he were half as smart as everyone said he was, should he enlighten her. Abruptly he was seized with the terrifying thought that Shaine might never fall in love with him. What would he do then?

Striving desperately for some kind of normality, Jake said, "Order an espresso—I'm planning on keeping you awake all night anyway."

"Are you all right? You look kind of funny," she said dubiously.

With relief, he spoke the truth. "I'm just happy to be here with you, Shaine."

How could he not be, when he was head over heels in love with her?

*   *   *

Jake bided his time all weekend, his body saying what he wasn't yet prepared to put into words. They ate, drank, danced, wandered the cobblestone streets hand in hand, and window-shopped. They laughed a lot, in bed and out. Because, of course, the other thing they did was spend hours in bed, and very little of it sleeping.

Shaine's new nightgown didn't get a lot of wear.

And then, all too soon, it was Sunday morning. Jake woke early. Propping himself up on one elbow, he ran his eyes over Shaine's sleeping face, his heart turning over with love. Before he left this morning, he had to know when he was going to see her again.

As though she sensed him watching her, she stretched, yawned and opened her eyes. "Good morning," she said sleepily.

"Our last morning here."

Emotions chased themselves across her face so rapidly he couldn't keep up. With a touch of desperation she pulled his head down and kissed him, her nails digging into his scalp. The result was entirely predictable. But the same thread of desperation ran through a lovemaking as intense as it was fast; and when it was done, she lay back on the pillows, avoiding his eyes. Jake said steadily, "What's the matter?"

"Nothing." She wrinkled her nose. "Back to ordinary living, I suppose."

"Will you miss me?" he said quietly.

With a teasing smile she tickled his ribs. "I'll miss this."

"Not just my body. All of me."

Her smile faded. "I don't know what you're getting at."

"This weekend has meant a lot to me. I want to know what it's meant for you."

How could she answer him when his big body was hovering over her, his blue eyes pinioning her to the bed?

"Jake, we've had the most incredible sex and a lot of fun, and you loved my new nightgown. Isn't that enough?"

He should never have started this; but it was too late now to back down. "When can I see you again?"

She raised her chin defiantly. "I come back to Montreal next March."

He forced his temper down. "Don't play games."

"There's no room in my life for wild weekends—you know what the cove's like. This was truly wonderful, and I figure I deserved every minute of it. But there can't be a repeat."

"So it was nothing but an escapade for you?"

"What's wrong with that?" She had no idea what this weekend meant for her. For thirty-six hours she'd flung off the constraints of thirteen years. She'd luxuriated in a man's body, allowed her sensuality full play, and had been certain in her bones that Jake had loved everything she'd done.

And now it was over.

How could she possibly know what it meant?

The words were past Jake's lips before he could stop them. "Shaine, I've fallen in love with you all over again. Or maybe I never fell out of love the first time."

She paled and sat up, crossing her arms over her breasts. "I don't want you to be in love with me!"

"Why not? You were happy enough when you were seventeen."

"Yes, I was," she said. "I might have been young and impressionable and full of romantic ideas—but you did make me happy. Very happy. And then you vanished, breaking off love and friendship as if they'd never been."

"We've been through all that," he said in a taut voice.

"Then let me tell you something else," she said edgily. "Six years later, when Daniel started school and I finally had some time to myself, I had an affair. His name was Kyle Manley, he was a hotel executive touring the coast to interview local businesses and restaurants. He was handsome and charming and I was starved for that kind of attention. So I fell for him, hard. And he, so he said, did the same.''

Knowing better than to touch her, Jake waited. ''We'd meet at the motel where he was staying. I always got home before Daniel did. And then one day I invited him for dinner so he could meet my son. He said he had a meeting that night up in St. Anthony, but he could come the next night. So I cooked a nice dinner and waited.'' She finished bitterly, ''You know the rest. Because, of course, he never came—I never heard from him again. He didn't want to meet my son. He just wanted me in the sack.''

''I'm sorry,'' Jake said inadequately.

''You see the pattern? For the second time in a row I got dumped. Abandoned. Left behind to pick up the pieces of my life.'' She took a deep breath, trying to work the tension out of her shoulders. ''Never again, Jake. Sure, right now it's amusing you to show me the high life and spend your money on me. But how long will that last?''

''What's between us is nothing to do with money!''

''Okay, okay. But don't you see where I'm coming from? You were in love with me and you left. Kyle said he loved me and he left. Now you're in love with me again. I don't even want to talk about it!'' She scrambled out of bed in a flash of bare limbs. ''I've got to shower and pack and get to the airport.''

Jake rolled off the bed and caught her around the wrist, his fingers like steel. ''Because of Daniel, I'm not going to disappear from your life. And I'm not done with this.''

''Well, I am!''

''Go shower,'' he said. ''I'll run you to the airport after breakfast.''

The bathroom door shut with a decisive snap. Jake threw his belongings in his case, furious with her, equally furious with himself. He should have waited. Built a relationship slowly, let her grow to trust him. But instead he'd rushed his fences.

If he ever met a hotel executive by the name of Kyle Manley, the guy was toast.

Somewhat cheered by that thought, Jake used the second bathroom to shower and get dressed. He and Shaine took the stairs down to the restaurant, where she buried her face in the newspaper. Jake picked up the business section. "Isn't this what long-married couples do—read the paper at breakfast?"

"I wouldn't know."

He slathered raspberry preserve on a crisp croissant. "I'm not going to go away. Not this time."

"I'll be sure and tell Daniel."

Thoroughbred racehorses, thought Jake, weren't for the faint of heart. "At least you're not indifferent to me," he said cheerfully. "Pass the cream, would you?"

She lowered the paper, frowning, and thrust the chased silver jug at him. "Next time I call a man for a wild weekend, I'll think twice."

"Put the knife in and then twist it, why don't you?"

Her face fell. She said helplessly, "I'm being such a bitch...I don't know how to handle this. I'm not sophisticated like all your other women."

"I'd noticed."

A ghost of a smile tilted her mouth. "You fell in love with me because of my homemade dress."

He leaned forward. "I fell in love with you because you're passionately involved in day-to-day living, and you're—what a tedious word, but I don't know a better one—dependable. I'd trust you with my life."

Shaken by the intensity of his feelings, he added, "Finish your coffee or...please don't cry, Shaine, I can't stand it when you do that."

She blinked back the tears that were clinging to her lashes. Then she glanced at her watch and gave a yelp of dismay. "I'm going to miss my plane. I'll have to take a cab, it'd be quicker."

"I'll take you to the airport and we'll be in plenty of time."

"You're much too used to giving orders."

"So are you. That'll give us lots to talk about when we're old and cranky."

Her eyes glittered dangerously. "Take a hint, Jake—lay off."

"No," he said.

She picked up her purse and marched across the dining room. Ten minutes later they were in the limousine he'd hired and on their way to Dorval airport. Once her bags were checked, Jake went with her to security. "I'll call you in a couple of days," he said. "I'm in Manhattan all week." Then he kissed her thoroughly and with considerable enjoyment. She emerged looking ruffled, utterly desirable and very cranky.

Flashing his best smile at her, Jake turned and walked away. He wished he felt half as confident as he looked.

CHAPTER ELEVEN

ON WEDNESDAY afternoon a truck delivered Shaine's semi-annual purchase of glass. She'd cleared her shelves, and once all the packages were in her studio, methodically started shelving the bright panes of cathedral and opalescent glass, checking them off on the invoice.

As she got near the bottom of the list, her hands stilled. Ring mottled glass, baroque glass, German antique glass...she hadn't ordered any of those. Couldn't afford to, much as she longed to work with them. Then she realized there was a note attached to the back of the invoice. Jake Reilly had purchased and paid for the added shipment. Last Friday, the day he'd arrived in Montreal.

She bit her lip. How had he known?

The glass was beautiful. The antique glass, in particular, was perfect for an abstract design she'd had in mind ever since she'd seen the craters of Cañadas.

He'd never mentioned this last night when he'd phoned.

She could send them back. Because wasn't she getting more and more deeply indebted to him? And wasn't that the last thing she wanted?

Then she heard Daniel dropping his schoolbooks in the back porch and kicking off his shoes. Hastily she hid the invoice on her desk, and with great care slid the first pane into its wooden slot.

"Hey, Mum, guess what?"

"You made ninety-nine in English."

"Not likely. The coach thinks I might get selected player of the year at the tournament next weekend."

"That's wonderful, Daniel."

"We leave Friday right after lunch."

"I'll make sure your stuff's ready."

"That's a neat color," Daniel said.

"They have such wonderful glass at the place in
Montreal," she said evasively, "that's why I keep going
back there."

"You could have gone to an NHL game, the Canadiens
were playing Saturday night."

On Saturday night she and Jake had made love in a tub
full of bubble bath. She bent over the next pane of glass.
"I'll stop and get dinner in a few minutes. Devlin gave us
some crabmeat."

They ate in the kitchen. As he scraped out the bottom of
the casserole, Daniel said, "This is nearly as good as those
prawns we all had at the resort."

Her mind more on her design than on dinner, Shaine said
absently, "Not as good as the steak he fed me Saturday—"
She broke off, aghast. "The last evening we were in New
York, is what I meant," she babbled, and remembered
she'd eaten roast pork that night.

Daniel's jaw dropped. "He was in Montreal with you."

She couldn't lie to him. "We did meet, yes. But he—"

"You never have dates. Or meet up with guys."

"I sometimes have dinner with Cameron," Shaine said.

"He doesn't count. How come you met up with my father? You must've planned it ahead of time."

"Daniel, this really isn't—"

"You going to marry him?"

"Never," Shaine said with more honesty than tact.

"Why not?"

"I don't want to marry anyone!"

"Has he asked you?"

"Yes. I said no. And that's the end of it."

"If he asked you, he must want to marry you."

"It takes two people to make a marriage," she said.
"I'm sorry I ever mentioned him."

Daniel's chair scraped the floor as he pushed himself to

his feet. His blue eyes blazing in a way that reminded her uncomfortably of his father, he said, "There's no reason you couldn't marry him—you guys get on okay, I was watching you the whole time we were away."

"You want me to marry him," she said in a dazed voice.

His color hectic, Daniel said choppily, "Everyone else's parents are married. But not you. You gotta be different."

"I can't get married just—"

"I don't want to talk about it anymore," Daniel muttered and ran from the room. A moment later the back door slammed.

Shaine buried her head in her hands. Why, oh why, hadn't she kept her mouth shut?

How could she have been so stupid?

This was a question Shaine was to repeat more than once through the week. Daniel, normally sunny-tempered, was morose and withdrawn, even on occasion downright rude. She did her best to keep her cool, but had to admit that when he left the house Friday morning for school and then the tournament, she was glad to see him go.

He'd come back in a different frame of mind, and life would go on the way it always had.

She spent all day Friday in the shop. On Saturday Jenny took the eight-hour shift, freeing Shaine to go to her studio, where the table was covered with sketches and color mockups for the abstract she was working on. Pushing Jake, Daniel and the cove out of her mind, she got to work.

When the doorbell rang, she was astounded to realize two hours had passed. Straightening her back, running her fingers through her hair, she went to the door. "Why, Mary," she said cordially, "how are you?"

Mary Bates was the mother of Art, Daniel's friend who was the goalie on the hockey team; she was also the wife of the junior coach, Hardy. "Fine," she said. "I just wanted to check on Daniel. Is he feeling better?"

"Feeling better?" Shaine repeated, wondering if the whole cove knew she and Daniel had been at odds all week.

"Hardy said he had the flu. That's why he couldn't go to the tournament."

Her eyes blank with shock, Shaine faltered, "You'd better come in—are you saying Daniel's not at the tournament?"

"That's right. Called Hardy yesterday morning and said he was too sick to go. Hardy wasn't best pleased but you can't fight the flu. You mean Daniel's not here?"

Shaine sat down on the nearest chair. "No," she said in a thin voice, "he's not here. Oh God, Mary, where's he gone?" Then, her brain racing and her stomach in an icy knot, she answered her own question. "He must have gone to find his father. We had a big fight on Wednesday—Daniel wants me to marry Jake and I said I couldn't."

"Where does Jake live?"

"New York City. Miles away." Gripped by a terror unlike any she'd ever felt, Shaine stammered, "Daniel's been gone since yesterday morning and I don't have any idea where he is. Or how to find him."

Mary said stoutly, "We'll check his room first to see if he left a note." But although the two of them searched high and low, they found nothing. Then Mary said, "Do you have Jake's phone number?"

"Yes. Of course. I—I'll get it."

Shaine's knees felt as though they wouldn't hold her weight, while her hands were shaking like poplar leaves in the wind. "Here it is," she said. "Mary, would you dial for me?"

What if Jake wasn't home? He could be anywhere from Queensland to Paris, and she'd have no way of reaching him. In cold fear she clutched the phone, counting the rings. On the fourth one, the receiver was picked up. "Jake Reilly."

Shaine collapsed into the chair. "Jake," she whispered.

"Shaine? What's wrong?"

"Daniel's run away," she said; her voice sounded as though it was coming from another woman.

"When?" Jake rapped.

"He found out about Montreal and we had a big fight. He was supposed to go to a hockey tournament yesterday morning but I only just discovered he didn't go. Oh, Jake, we've got to find him!"

"You think he's on his way here?"

"He wants me to marry you," she said wretchedly. "I don't know where else he'd go."

"Okay. I'll get onto it right away. You're not to worry, Shaine, he's a smart kid and he'll stay out of trouble. Is there someone with you?"

"Yes," she gulped. "Will you call me as soon as you hear anything?"

"I'll have him traced. What time does the bus leave the cove on Fridays?"

"Nine-thirty—of course, that's what he must have done, I'm not thinking straight."

"Give me their number. Then pour yourself a glass of brandy and stay by the phone. We'll find him, I promise."

She could feel his certainty enfold her almost as if he were standing in the kitchen. "I let it drop you were in Montreal," she blurted. "It's my fault."

"I'm as much to blame as you are," he said shortly. "Talk to you soon."

Very carefully she replaced the receiver in its slot. Mary, in the meantime, had put on the kettle. With a watery smile Shaine said, "Jake suggested brandy. But I think tea's a better idea."

The minutes crept by, until an hour had passed since she'd talked to Jake, then an hour and a half, then two. When she was almost at the point of total panic, the bell shrilled. Her nerves jangling, her shoulders rigid as iron bars, she picked up the phone.

"He's on the bus coming into the city," Jake said tersely. "They've been alerted and I'll go and meet it. I'll call you as soon as he's at my place—don't worry if it's a couple more hours, I need to talk to him and find out what's going on."

"All right," Shaine said, dropped the phone, put her head down on the table and sobbed as though her heart was broken. Mary picked up the receiver, and from a long way away Shaine heard her say, "She'll be all right, she's just a little upset. Good work, Jake. Yes, I'll stay with her." There was a pause, then Mary finished, "Okay, I've got all that, and I'll make sure she gets there. 'Bye, Jake."

Mary put down the phone, wrapped her arms around her friend and held on tight. "Everything's going to be fine," she said.

The bus station, eddying with people, wasn't a place Jake would want to see Daniel on his own. Welcome to fatherhood, he thought, as he waited at the bay for the bus to pull in. It hadn't been that difficult to track the boy down, although he was wondering how Daniel had gotten across the border on his own. He'd soon find out, he thought with a touch of grimness, Shaine's terrible sobbing echoing in his ears.

The bus arrived with a hiss of brakes. The door opened and the passengers straggled out, waiting on the concrete siding to get their baggage. Then Daniel came down the steps. Jake saw the boy take a hunted look around; he looked both young and out of his depth, neither of which was a good idea in a city that had more than its share of predators.

Jake stepped forward. "Daniel," he said.

His son's head swung around. Unmistakably, relief was his predominant emotion, followed quickly by a mixture of fear and defiance. Jake gave him a quick hug. "Do you have a bag?"

Daniel indicated his bulging backpack. "Just this."

"Let's get out of here. We'll talk when we get to the condo."

Within half an hour Jake was closing the door behind them. "Hungry?" he said shrewdly.

Daniel gave a great sigh. "Once I paid for my ticket, I didn't have enough money left for food."

"Come into the kitchen and we'll see what we can find."

Daniel demolished a pizza, two glasses of milk, a banana and four cookies. Eying Jake warily, he said, "Can I call my mum?"

"She knows you're here. I'd rather talk to you first."

"You gotta change her mind!" Daniel burst out.

"Explain yourself."

"She told me you guys were together in Montreal and that you'd asked her to marry you but she said no. I don't get it—she likes you okay, why won't she marry you?"

"You came all this way to ask me that?"

Daniel slumped in his chair, scowling at the table. "I want her and you to get married."

Suppressing the urge to smooth the frown from his son's face, Jake said, "Why, Daniel?"

"All the other kids, their parents are married."

"So you want to be the same as everyone else?" Jake said gently. "Is that it?"

Systematically, Daniel was cracking his knuckles. Almost inaudibly, he mumbled, "I want a father."

A father. Trying hard to keep any emotion out of his voice, Jake said, "Would anyone do?"

Daniel looked up, his blue eyes full of misery. "You're my father. You're the one I want."

Jake stood up, lifted Daniel to his feet and put his arms around him. As the boy started to cry, he held him tightly, his heart overflowing with love, his own eyes pricking with tears. He said unsteadily, "I want to be a real father to you, Daniel. More than I can say."

Daniel looked up, scrubbing at his wet cheeks. "Then you gotta change her mind," he repeated unanswerably.

Jake ruffled the boy's hair, opting for one part of the truth. "She believes she can't take you away from the cove. Your home's there, your uncles, the hockey team...so she thinks you both have to live there."

"That's kinda dumb," Daniel said slowly.

"But it is your home...want some pop?"

"Yeah, thanks." The boy's brow furrowed. "I liked being here in the city. The cove's not the same since we went away with you—it's smaller, like."

Jake knew the feeling. He said calmly, "We were on vacation, remember, Daniel. It wasn't real life, the day-to-day stuff like going to school in a big city where you don't know anyone."

Daniel shrugged. "I'm cool at making friends. And I can fight if I have to. Uncle Padric taught me some down and dirty stuff in case I ever needed it. Some of the kids used to call Mum names 'cause she's not married—so I had to show 'em I wouldn't stand for that."

Hit by a wave of huge remorse, Jake said, "I'm sorry you had to do that."

"No big deal." Daniel's face lit up. "I could maybe go to those practices if we lived here."

"You could be on the team," Jake said. "The coach called me afterward, they're always on the lookout for new talent."

"If we lived here, we'd go back to the cove sometimes, wouldn't we?"

"Of course we would. But it might not be the same— you'd grow away from your friends and their lives would go on without you."

"Mum liked being away, too. She could do more glass stuff here than she can back home."

Jake knew he wasn't going to discuss with his son Shaine's determination never to marry anyone, least of all himself. "I'll talk to your mother, I promise—she's on her way here now, I arranged for the jet to pick her up in Deer Lake. I want both of you to see my place in the Hamptons, it's where I go when I need to get out of the city."

"Another house?" Daniel said, wide-eyed.

Refusing to be deflected, Jake said, "She was upset when you ran away. Which brings me to what else I have to say. Running away doesn't solve anything, Daniel. I ran away from the cove thirteen years ago, and robbed the three of us of all those years we could have had together. This time, it turned out fine for you—but you frightened your mother very badly, and I won't tolerate that."

"I forged her signature on a letter, snuck into the lawyer's office and put his seal on it," Daniel said in a rush. "He leaves it sitting on his desk all the time. That's how I got across the border."

True confessions, thought Jake, the rebel in his own spirit rather impressed by the boy's enterprise. "You must never do that again," he said sternly, and knew this as another of those moments when he crossed into the country called fatherhood. "Promise?"

"Yeah, I promise…she'll be mad," Daniel said gloomily.

But the first thing Shaine did when Jake and Daniel met his plane at the airport was to fling her arms around her son and hold him so tightly he could scarcely breathe. Then she looked right at him, blinking back tears, and said fiercely, "You lied to me. You frightened me out of my wits. If you ever even think of running away again, Daniel Seamus O'Sullivan, I'll throw you into ten fathoms of water trussed up in a herring net."

"Sorry, Mum," Daniel gulped.

"You'd better be sorry. The coach has grounded you for the next three games."

As Daniel's face fell, she said, "Running away is the

coward's way out. No O'Sullivan is a coward. Neither is a Reilly. You'd do well to remember that."

"Dad said the same thing."

Dad... The small word hung in the air. Shaine saw Jake's face change, and felt one more strand tightening around her. She wasn't going to ask Daniel why he'd run away. She knew the answer already. He wanted more of Jake than she was willing to provide.

Jake said calmly, "We're heading for my place in the Hamptons, Shaine, I want you and Daniel to see it. There's a snack in the car to hold you over until we get there."

"It's a Ferrari, Mum. A silver Ferrari. I sat in the front seat on the way to the airport, but you can have it now."

Recognizing this both as amends and a real sacrifice, Shaine did sit in the front as they worked their way west to Route 27 and the South Fork of Long Island. Neither she nor Jake had much to say to each other. His jawline had never looked so uncompromising, his profile so unyielding. She tried to steel herself against the conflict she knew was coming; and, with an equal lack of success, against the charm of historic whaling villages, the long stretch of pale sand, and the increasingly luxurious homes of New York's wealthy.

But it was Jake's house that captivated her. It was set in a small inlet, with its own secluded beach and mooring, yet with access to the rolling Atlantic surf. The house with its mansard roof, stone facings and mullioned windows twinkling in the setting sun seemed to welcome her with open arms. Late roses scented the air around the heavy oak door; the gardens called to the artist within her.

Jake said casually, "Do you like it?"

"I love it," she breathed. "It's beautiful."

She meant it, he thought in deep relief. "I've only had the place three years. I haven't spent as much time as I should have on the interior...let's go in." He then took them on a quick tour. The sunroom overlooking the ocean;

the vast attic that would make an ideal studio; the balcony off the master bedroom with its view of scarlet maples and spruce on the far shore and the smooth waters of the inlet: all the while, he watched Shaine's dazzled face.

He wanted her here in the house that had called to him from the first moment he'd seen it.

He was going to do his utmost to get what he wanted.

The housekeeper had left pasta, fresh rolls and salad for dinner, with a delicious fruit flan. By the time they'd eaten, Daniel was openly yawning, and made no protest when Jake took him upstairs. "Your mum's next door," Jake said easily, "and I'm down the hall. We'll have to head back tomorrow so you don't miss any more school. Sleep well, son."

Daniel grinned, punched him lightly on the arm and closed the door of his room. Jake went downstairs. Shaine was sitting in the octagonal alcove by the herb garden, the gurgle of the creek falling softly through the open window. He pulled her to her feet. Letting his heart spill over into his kiss, he held her close. "I've been wanting to do that ever since you stepped off the jet," he said. "You've had a long day, Shaine."

She tilted her head back, her green eyes challenging. "It's not over yet, is it?"

He sat down across from her, pouring himself another glass of wine. A normal, romantic proposal of marriage was out of the question. Shaine didn't love him. Choosing his words, he said, "Daniel's running away was a wake-up call. You heard him call me Dad—he wants a regular family, a mother and a father who are married to each other and live together."

"We don't always get what we want," she said evenly.

Jake quelled a flicker of rage. "In this case, we can give him what he wants. You'll marry me, Shaine."

"I won't!"

As if she hadn't spoken, he went on, "The condo would

be our home base. I can easily cut back on the amount of traveling I do, so that I'm around to be a proper, live-in father. You could have a studio out here, and rent another one in the city, if you need to. You're more than ready for change artistically, you know that as well as I do."

"Are you trying to buy me?"

"I'm merely listing the advantages to you of a step that's inevitable."

"Daniel belongs in Cranberry Cove. Not here."

"I talked to him about that today, too. He's been seeing the cove with different eyes since our trip, and he's more than willing to try something new."

She paled. "Leave his uncles and all his friends?"

"We can go back for visits anytime, and there's no reason your three brothers can't visit us here. Daniel assured me he's good at making friends, and thanks to Padric he knows how to stave off bullies. Despite his escapade this weekend, he's got a good head on his shoulders—he's a credit to you."

"Jake, this is all very clever of you," she blazed, "but you're forgetting one thing. I don't want to get married."

"But we don't always get what we want—didn't you just say that?"

Her breath hissed between her teeth. "Just you listen to me for a minute—and listen hard because I'm only saying this once. I've never told you what it was like for me after you left. The very first days, when I kept expecting you to call or write, and you didn't—when I started to wonder what you'd meant by the word love. Worrying about my mother as she went through surgery. Then realizing my cycle was off, and going to see Doc. Pregnant and abandoned—what a cliché that is, and how horribly lonely and frightening it is when you're actually living through it. Not telling my parents until my mother had finished the radiation."

Because it was suddenly imperative to know, Jake said,

"Did you ever think of an abortion?" As she shook her head vehemently, he added, "Why not?"

She looked at him as though he had two heads. "It was our baby, Jake. Yours and mine."

"So you did love me," he said slowly.

She sighed, gazing down at her hands and knowing it was time for the truth. "Yes, I did. I lied to you on Ghost Island all those years ago because I didn't know how else to send you away. And I've been lying to you ever since you came back. I loved you with all my heart…probably from that day you found me crying about Sally Hatchet's birthday party."

Jake felt as if a huge weight had been lifted from his chest. "I wish you'd told me the truth…back then, and more recently."

"I did what I thought was best."

She hadn't told him why she'd lied. "What happened when your parents found out you were pregnant?"

"They insisted I go off to university and that they'd bring the baby up. They knew it wouldn't fool anyone in the cove—but they also knew how desperate I was to get away. By the end of the summer, the specialist said Mum's prognosis was good. So off I went. Daniel was born very conveniently in the March break. My mother took him home and I went back to classes. For two whole weeks I went to lectures and passed in assignments and tried to put my heart into it."

Her voice shook in spite of herself. "But I couldn't live without Daniel. So I phoned them and said I was coming home to stay. They weren't very happy with me but they knew I meant it. The next day was the accident, and the rest you know."

"If only I could undo my actions," Jake said in a low voice. "If only I'd been there for you, Shaine."

She was playing with her fork, strain in every line of her body. "I'm not finished. My pregnancy should have been joyful—but instead it was full of anxiety and unhappiness. When I went into labor and you weren't there, I've never felt such a black loneliness. When our son was born, you weren't at my side. Jake, don't you see? The scars went deep. Too deep. And then the death of my parents meant that in the midst of mourning them I had to stay in the cove and bring up my brothers and my son. I did it, to the best of my ability. But it cost me. I can't just turn back the clock and say, Sure, I'll marry you, Jake, and I'll trust you to be there for me for the rest of my life. The betrayal went too deep."

She was telling truths that were all too real; his heart cold, Jake said, "When did you fall out of love with me?"

She got up, going to stand by the window, her fingers restlessly playing with the iron catch. "That didn't just happen—I worked at it. As Daniel grew up, I had a constant reminder of you in front of me every moment of every day. The same blue eyes, the same dark hair. I couldn't afford to stay in love with you, it was too painful. So I killed my love for you. I deliberately banished it from my life. It was the only way I could survive."

Jake gazed down at his clenched fists, the tendons tight as overstretched rope. He was too late. That's what she was saying. Years too late. And how could he blame her for doing everything within her power in order to survive?

Moving like a much older man, he got up, too. Standing behind her, he looked out into the shadowed garden, his hands heavy on her shoulders. He couldn't give up. He wouldn't. She was too important. Too essential. "I can't prove I'll always be there for you," he said. "The only way to do that is for the two of us to live together for the rest of our lives. But I swear by all that's holy that I'll never abandon you again. Never."

Her head drooped, her nape a pale, vulnerable curve. "Something died in me all those years ago. I can't bring it to life again just because you and Daniel want me to."

He was losing her. Jake tightened his grip, swinging her around to face him. "We can't think about ourselves here. This is about Daniel."

"He and I were doing fine until you came back!"

He fought down pain coupled with an anger that was directed at himself as much as at her. "We're going to get married, Shaine. We'll share a bed and a life and our son. There's no other choice."

"You're still in love with me," she said stonily. "You'll get hurt."

"Let me worry about that." He managed a smile. "There are those who'd say I deserved it."

"It doesn't feel right, Jake," she whispered. "It just doesn't feel right."

With all the force of his willpower, he said, "It will. It has to. I love you so much, and we both love our son." He dropped his arms to his sides, his fists clenched in frustration. "If only I could take you to bed right now and just hold on to you…but I can't, not with Daniel here."

"No, you can't," she said steadily.

"We'll get married at the cove. In a week. I'll look after all the paperwork."

"You're riding over me as though I don't exist!"

"I don't know what else to do." Which was, he thought unhappily, the simple truth. For a mathematical genius who'd made several fortunes, he was doing one hell of a poor job in the emotional department. He added with savage emphasis, "I can't bear the thought of Daniel being bullied in the schoolyard."

Her shoulders slumped. "That's what really counts, isn't it? Daniel." Staring out of the window into the darkness, as though the dense shadows of the trees might offer her a place to hide, she said tonelessly, "You win. We'll tell Daniel tomorrow morning."

But as Jake reached out for her, she flinched away from him. Her gesture tore him to the heart. *You'll get hurt,* she'd said. He hadn't expected she'd be proven right so soon and so painfully.

"Go to bed, Shaine," he said. "You look exhausted."

He watched her trail out of the room; and perhaps the most painful realization of all was that he'd crushed her spirit. Defeated her.

He'd gotten what he wanted. But at what cost?

CHAPTER TWELVE

ONE week later, the day before Jake was due to arrive to marry her, Shaine found herself unable to stay in the house with her own thoughts a minute longer. She'd been cooped up all day because a storm was raging outside; according to the radio, it was the tail end of a hurricane. She was quite prepared to believe this from the violence of wind and rain that had battered the village all day.

She had the house to herself; Daniel had been invited to Art's birthday party, and was to stay overnight at Mary and Hardy's. Dragging on her rain jacket, she found her rubber boots. She'd go as far as the woodshed and watch the surf for a while. Maybe it would calm her down.

If she was a normal, sensible woman, she'd stay in her kitchen and make herself a cup of tea. The radio had also claimed this was the worst storm in years.

Nature's excesses had always beckoned her; and hadn't some of her best work come from pushing her limits both outdoors and in?

Marrying Jake was pushing her limits.

Scowling, she pushed open the door, grabbed it as it tried to fly out of her hand, and jammed it shut behind her. Pellets of rain and driven spray stung her face; the wind flattened her jacket to her body. Head down, she pushed her way toward the woodshed, already feeling better. At least here she knew what she was struggling against.

Waves reared from the sea like great white stallions, their manes of foam strung out by the gale. The noise was deafening. Exhilarated, momentarily forgetting her sore heart and tangled nerves, Shaine battled her way beyond the shed. She'd go as far as the first cove, where she could watch the water slam into the rocks.

In the cove, wave collided with wave and spray hissed against granite; great sheets of marbled water flung themselves at the face of the cliff, only to slide back in a tumble of foam. Shaine curled her fingers around the trunk of an embattled spruce, fighting for balance. If she went just a little further, she might catch a glimpse of Ghost Island. The surf there should be magnificent.

Her boots slopped through water that in places was ankle-deep. Hands deep in her pockets, she licked her lips where fresh water and salt were mingling. Like tears, she thought with a superstitious shiver, and remembered how many tears she had shed in those first weeks after Jake had left the cove.

She wasn't going to think about Jake. She'd been thinking about him all day. Enough was enough.

The inshore reefs had vanished under huge waves that rolled imperiously toward the cliffs. High tide, she thought, and hoped Devlin's boat was well moored to the lee of the wharf.

She was halfway to the rocks; she should turn back. A cup of tea was beginning to seem like a very good idea, particularly as her waterproof jacket was no longer living up to its claim. Besides, her hands were cold.

Then, at the edge of the cliff, she noticed a clump of flowers, their small purple bells bowed into the dirt. On impulse she stepped closer, stooping to pick them so she could enjoy them indoors. And felt the ground move beneath her feet.

For a split second she thought she was imagining that eerie sensation of having nothing firm to stand on. Wasn't that how she'd been feeling for days, ever since she'd come back from Jake's beautiful house in the Hamptons? But then, in a shaft of terror, she realized that the edge of the cliff was breaking loose, weakened by rain and spray. She

grabbed for the nearest clump of grass. It slipped through
her wet fingers; with a cry of fear she felt herself sliding
inexorably downward. Desperately she lunged for the nearest juniper, her boots scrabbling for a hold in a mix of mud
and stones. Then she was skidding in the mud, rocks scrap-
ing her palms and her cheek.

Below her, the ocean roared with primeval rage.

Daniel, she thought. Oh God, Daniel…and Jake. Jake
whom she loved.

With an impact that jarred her whole body, Shaine's feet
slammed into a boulder. Stones skittered past her, to plunge
into the sea. The mud was cold, glued to her face. But she
had stopped falling.

Her breath sobbing in her lungs, her nails digging for a
hold, she flattened herself to the cliff face. Her heart was
hammering against her ribs; she knew panic was only seconds away, and fought it down with all her willpower. Very
carefully, she looked downward.

Her eyes winced away from the melee of water. Her
boots had hit an outcrop of granite, large enough and well
enough wedged into the cliff to support her weight.

Barring another mudslide, she was safe.

But how long before anyone came to look for her?
Daniel wouldn't be home tonight. Jake wasn't arriving until
tomorrow. There was no reason why Devlin, Padric or
Connor should call on her.

Did she have the strength to last here all night? To stay
awake so that she wouldn't tumble from the rock into the
sea?

With another whimper of fear, Shaine laid her cheek to
the cliff. Jake, she thought. Somehow Jake would send
help. Because he loved her. As she, of course, loved him.

She closed her eyes and her ears, willing away the savage
waves and the wicked shrieks of the wind. Wasn't Jake
both the storm she was driven to enter and the safe harbor
she craved?

She'd never stopped loving him; it had taken a hurricane and a mudslide to show her that. She'd tried, heaven knows. She'd fought against her love, and had, eventually, convinced herself that she'd exiled him completely from her life. That he no longer meant anything to her.

That's what she'd told him in that peaceful little room overlooking the inlet, and that's what she'd believed to be true.

But she'd been wrong. Only now, terrified that she might die before she could tell him she loved him, did she realize how deluded she'd been. Her love for Jake was the underlying current of her life, the ocean in which she swam, the wind through her soul.

Her cold fingers tightened their grip. She had to tell him. She had to. She couldn't bear for him to go through the rest of his life thinking she'd destroyed the love they'd once shared.

She let her mind drift back to that lovely octagonal room. She and Jake were eating breakfast in the early morning sunlight. They'd made love in the night, and that memory was there in their faces and their bodies. And then Daniel slouched into the room, hungry as always, his casual grin speaking of an underlying happiness that his mother and his father loved each other, and that all three of them were making a home together...

Jake was driving down Breakheart Hill into Cranberry Cove. His car radio was rattling on about Hurricane Brenda. Jake wasn't about to argue. Fighting to keep his vehicle on his side of the road, through driving sheets of rain he caught glimpses of the barrens, stained scarlet by the blueberry shrubs, and of feathery gold tamaracks flailing in the wind. Welcome home, he thought wryly.

He'd come a day early, thinking he'd arrive before the storm. But he'd been wrong.

This was Saturday. He and Shaine were getting married

on Monday. Tomorrow his mother and stepfather were arriving from Sydney to help celebrate his wedding.

Celebrate, he thought. It didn't seem like the right word. Although his mother had been predictably delighted to hear he was getting married.

Would he ever forget Daniel's lopsided grin when they'd told him about the wedding? The way the boy had hugged him? He had to hold on to that. Because ever since that Saturday night in the Hamptons, Shaine had felt a million miles away.

As he'd made his way through a maze of documents and details, she'd been cooperative and cold as ice. That she was regretting her decision to marry him was evident. She'd assured him she was acting like a happy prospective bride with Daniel and her brothers; but when she was talking to him, Jake, on the phone late at night, the front dropped and her true feelings came out.

Was he making the worst mistake in his life, an even worse one than his precipitate departure from the cove all those years ago? Was forcing Shaine to marry him a risk he shouldn't take?

He crept along the deserted village streets. The power was on; the yellow gleam of lights through an afternoon as gloomy as dusk was oddly comforting. Shaine's house was also lit up. Every muscle in his body tight with tension, Jake parked, grabbed his briefcase and ran for the door.

He didn't bother knocking. Swiping rain from his face, his jeans in that short distance plastered to his legs, he opened the kitchen door and called, "Shaine? It's Jake."

She wasn't home; he knew it instantly. Refusing to see this as a premonition, he shucked off his shoes and went into the kitchen, where he found a note Daniel had taped to the refrigerator. Daniel was invited to an overnight birthday party on Saturday for his friend Art and had finished off the loaf of raisin bread and the leftover corned beef hash.

Today was Saturday. Jake's spirits lifted. They were doing this for Daniel. He had to remember that.

Where was Shaine? He hadn't planned to arrive until tomorrow, so she wasn't expecting him. She could be anywhere in the village.

Her car, he remembered, had been parked by the house. So she was somewhere close. Checking, he saw that her rain jacket was gone from the back porch, as were her rubber boots. On impulse he picked up the phone and dialed Devlin's number. "She was planning on being home," Devlin said, puzzled. "She wanted to work on a project in her studio. I'll call around and see if I can find her."

Shaine's studio was a litter of sketches, the photos she'd taken of the craters on Tenerife spread among them. Jake could almost sense her presence, and felt a chill travel his spine. She was drinking tea with a neighbor. Of course she was.

Rain slashed the windowpanes, the gale moaning around the eaves. Repetitively, a loose shingle scraped at the roof. Like fingernails scrabbling for a hold, thought Jake, and in sudden cold terror knew Shaine was in trouble.

The telephone rang, making him start. "Can't seem to find her anywhere," Devlin said. "But I'll keep trying. She didn't seem herself the last while, I'll say that...but not even my crazy sister would be out on the cliffs in this kind of blow."

"I'm going out there to check," Jake said. "If I'm not back in half an hour, come looking for me, will you?"

"Will do," Devlin said with a lack of surprise that sharpened Jake's sense of urgency. Zipping up his jacket, grabbing the biggest flashlight on the porch, he stepped out into the storm.

He knew every inch of the cliff path. But the rain blinded him, the wind playing with him as if he were weightless; underfoot, the ground was sodden, the last flowers flattened and crushed. He struggled on, pausing every now and then to shout Shaine's name, his voice tossed out to sea like the scream of a wounded gull.

She couldn't be out here.

But wasn't this the place she always came for comfort? For strength?

His unease deepened. He pushed it down as he passed the cove with its lashing waves and seethe of foam. He'd go as far as the clump of granite rocks where he'd first confronted Shaine with the knowledge that Daniel was his son; then he'd turn back. In the meantime, Devlin would have left a message to say Shaine was visiting a friend.

He was making a fool of himself venturing out on the cliffs in a hurricane. Was he equally a fool to make Shaine marry him? One of the things he loved most about her was her fiery spirit. So what was he trying to do? Tame her to his will? Break that spirit?

That would be the cruelest thing he could do to her.

Tripping over a tussock of grass because he wasn't watching where he was going, Jake swore under his breath and toiled on. He'd have to talk to her. Surely, between them, they could work something out.

Directly ahead of him the path had been washed away, disappearing in a tumble of rocks, exposed mud and uprooted grass. His heart slammed in his chest, all his premonitions coalescing into an overwhelming dread. He approached the crevasse with exquisite care. Dropping to his knees, he peered over the edge.

A woman in a blue rain jacket was clinging to the face of the cliff, her feet anchored on an outcrop of boulders. Below her, the waves heaved themselves upward and surf swarmed the rocks. He tried to shout her name, but his voice was caught in his throat.

Then Shaine looked up, her face a pale oval in the gathering darkness. Although Jake could see her lips moving, he couldn't distinguish her words through the howling wind. His eyes like gimlets, he sought a pathway through the mud and loose rocks, a way of reaching her; and found nothing. If he tried to slide down the cliff toward her, there was a huge risk he'd start another mudslide, sending both of them to their deaths on the rocks below. Even if he was successful in landing on the granite outcrop, there was no chance the two of them could climb up to safety. No footholds. No handholds. And always, waiting for them, the wild and hungry sea.

He had to leave her alone and get help.

Had he ever made a more difficult decision in his life?

Cupping his hands around his mouth, he yelled, "I'll go for help. Hold on—I'll be as quick as I can. Shaine, I love you."

Did she smile at him? He couldn't tell. He hated leaving her alone and in such danger; it tore the heart from his chest. But there was no other choice.

Backing away from the ugly tear in the ground, he got to his feet and started to run. Devlin would have ropes. Connor would help. And Padric, he thought, would curse the broken leg that condemned him to inactivity.

Jake pounded along the path, splashing through the puddles; and as he ran, he focused all his energy on Shaine. Hang on, he prayed. Be safe. Daniel needs you, and so do I. Oh God, so do I.

As he rounded the woodshed, he saw Devlin coming down the steps of Shaine's house. Jake grabbed the other man by the sleeve and tugged him into the shed out of the wind. His breath heaving in his chest, he gasped, "We need ropes—she's partway down the cliff, there was a mudslide."

"There's rope in my car. I'll call Connor and get him over here along with some of his buddies. Is she hurt?"

"I don't think so."

"The first-aid kit's in the back porch."

Within five minutes Jake, Devlin, Connor and two burly friends of Connor's were heading back along the path. Jake set a killing pace; it still felt like forever before they arrived at the mudslide. He knelt by the edge of the crevasse and with a great thud of his pulse saw the woman clinging like a limpet to the cliff face. Her upturned face swamped him with such a wave of emotion that he was momentarily dizzy.

Using his fisherman's skill with knots, Devlin quickly fashioned a harness from the rope he'd brought. Then he, Jake and Connor lowered it over the cliff. It blew from one side to the other, catching in the mud; his heart in his mouth, Jake watched Shaine grab for it, miss it and almost lose her balance. But on the second try, she brought the harness in close to her body. Leaning into the cliff, she inched it over her shoulders to her waist. Then she signaled with one hand.

"Okay, guys," Devlin said, only the faintest catch in his voice revealing his tension. "Move back from the edge real slow and pull like you never pulled in your life."

Shaine's hands had grasped the rope, which was also cinched around her waist; from his stance near the edge, Jake could only imagine her feet leaving the safety of the boulder and dangling in the air. He leaned backward, pulling with all his might. She was being lifted with agonizing slowness; he hated to think how the rope must be digging into her flesh.

The muscles in his arms and shoulders tightened unbearably. But step by step the five men were moving away from the cliff, deeper and deeper into the grass. Where the ropes were sawing into the mud, rocks broke loose, to tumble to the sea.

Devlin yelled, "Hold 'er there, boys. Jake, check on Shaine, see how close she is."

Her face was only three feet from the edge. Jake waved for the men to start pulling again, and added his own strength to the taut yellow rope, the skin on his palms burning. As one boot skidded in the wet grass, he dug his heels in and pulled still harder. And then Shaine was wriggling over the edge and moments later was lying facedown on the grass. Jake dropped the rope, seized her by the waist and tugged her well away from the cliff.

His breathing harsh in his ears, he eased the harness from her body. "Shaine," he gasped, "are you hurt?"

She shook her head. She too was fighting for breath, her cheeks filthy with mud, her hair darkened by the rain and clinging to her scalp. Jake gathered her close, pressing her face into his chest, overwhelmed with gratitude that she was alive and in his arms.

It could so easily have been otherwise.

Devlin shouted, "We should get her home. I'll go ahead and get hold of Doc."

Connor helped Jake to his feet. Holding Shaine in his arms, Connor ahead of him, Jake stumbled toward the cluster of houses with their yellow-lit windows.

Two hours later, Jake and Shaine were finally alone in the house. When they'd first arrived, she'd insisted on phoning Daniel, not wanting him to hear what had happened from anyone else, and had assured him that he should stay at the party. After Doc had checked her over and cleaned her scrapes, he'd lectured her about foolhardiness and taken his leave. Devlin and Connor had then, more colorfully, repeated Doc's message. She'd thanked them all, listening to their unflattering assessments of her character with a meekness that had amused Jake.

He went to the door with Devlin, who was the last to leave. "Thanks," Jake said roughly.

Devlin grinned at him, cuffing him on the shoulder. "See you at the wedding," he said. "I don't get my good suit out for everyone."

The door closed behind him. Jake, who didn't want any interruptions, took the precaution of locking it. Then he went upstairs to Shaine's bedroom. He had no idea what he was going to say to her; but he couldn't bear for her to be out of his sight for even a minute.

She was lying back on the pillows, her hair a tangle of curls, her cheeks still too pale. Her flowered cotton night-gown could have belonged to a maiden aunt. As she smiled at him, Jake's heart turned over with love. He dropped onto the bed, seized her hands in his and buried his face in her lap. No power in the world could have stopped the shudders that racked him from head to toe.

Shaine curved her body over his, her forehead resting on his shoulder. "It's all right, I'm safe," she whispered. "You saved my life, Jake—I don't think I could have hung on all night."

He fought back the nightmare images. The clutch of her fingers was real; she was safe, in her own bed. He kissed the pulse on her wrist in a passion of gratitude, striving to pull back from emotions so strong they frightened him. "You must be hungry," he muttered, pushing himself up and managing a smile. "Daniel appears to have left some homemade soup in the refrigerator—what was the matter, didn't he like it?"

"The soup can wait," she said. "There's something I have to tell you."

She was going to ask him to cancel the wedding; he knew it. He kept her hand in his, playing with the slender, capable fingers where dirt was still ground under her nails. "It's okay—I've figured out on my own that I shouldn't have bulldozed you into this wedding. I'm really sorry, I just wasn't thinking straight. We'll cancel it and we'll work something out, surely we can do that between us. Whatever happens, I swear I'll do my best to be a good father to Daniel and to support you in any way I can."

Pressing his lips into her palm, feeling the warmth of her skin, he added, "Thank God I came a day early. If you'd fallen and drowned...I don't know how I'd have lived with-out you. Because I love you more than I can say, that hasn't changed." He smiled straight into her eyes. "Probably never will."

"I don't want to cancel the wedding."

"Years ago you sacrificed your happiness for your mother's sake. Now you're about to do it for Daniel's. You mustn't. I want you to come willingly into my heart and my life—I can't force you."

She pushed herself up on the pillows, wincing from the soreness in her arms. "You're not listening to me."

"Homemade soup, that's what you need," Jake said.

Her green eyes sparking fire, she said, "Will you please shut up? I'm trying to tell you I've come to my senses and all you can do is blather on about homemade soup!"

"I'm the one who's come to his senses."

Temper tinged her cheeks with color. "I love you, Jake Reilly, and if you'd just get that fact through your thick head, I'll eat a whole saucepan of soup."

"You don't love me," he said blankly.

"I do so."

"You don't look as though you love me. You look as though you'd like to drop me off the cliff."

"It was while I was clinging to that damned cliff that I realized I'd been lying to myself for years. I'd killed any love I'd ever felt for you, that's what I believed. It was dead. Kaput. Over and done with." Her face suddenly anguished, she took his hand in hers, her nails digging into his skin. "But I was wrong. I never stopped loving you. How could I? You were my life. You still are. If you want to marry me on Monday, I'd really like that."

Scarcely believing his ears, Jake looked down at their intertwined fingers. "You love me?" he repeated. "You're sure?"

"There's nothing like being suspended over hurricane-force waves with your face in the mud to make you realize what's important," she said vigorously. "Are you going to make me get down on my knees and beg you to marry me?

I might be able to get down—but I'm not so sure I could get back up again.''

"Shaine, dearest Shaine, you're more than I deserve and yes, I'll marry you on Monday." Very gently, he eased her up from the pillows and put his arms around her, the heat of her body seeping through the thin cotton of her gown. "I love you," he said unsteadily. "Dear heart, I love you so much."

"That's good," she said contentedly, and kissed him full on the mouth.

It was by no means the kiss of a woman who considered herself an invalid. Jake pulled free, his pulses racing. "Keep that up and there'll be two of us in this bed. I'm going downstairs to heat the soup."

"You've got a fixation about that soup," she said with a mischievous gleam in her eyes. "Don't lean on my right hip, it's sore, and don't grab me by the shoulders—they're more than sore. But the rest of me, I assure you, is in fine working order." Her features radiant, she said, "Make love to me, Jake—now that we're going to be happily married. What a fool I was to believe I didn't love you any-more…underneath it all, I was so frightened that you'd leave me again."

"Never," Jake vowed, and knew this was the moment of real commitment, more so than any marriage vows. "Body and soul, I'm yours, Shaine."

"And I, yours," she said.

He traced the delicate bones of her wrist, where her pulse was fluttering beneath his thumb, and felt happiness course through his own veins. "I don't know how we're going to get that very modest nightgown over your head without you raising your arms."

"Ouch," said Shaine. "Let's do it fast."

"There's no hurry," Jake said, the wonderment in his face filling her with joy. "We've got a whole lifetime to-gether."

"And Daniel won't be back until tomorrow morning."
She glanced at him through her lashes, her cheeks tinged
with pink. "Daniel has let it be known that he wouldn't
mind having a brother or a sister. So he could teach him—
or her, I must have done something right—to play hockey."

Jake chuckled. "And would you like that?"

"Yes," she said. "You by my side loving me as I need
to be loved, and a baby on the way…that would make me
extraordinarily happy."

"Then we'll work on it," he said, and very gently lifted
the nightgown over her head. His own clothes were soon
thrown to the floor. In her bed, his arms around her naked
body, her eager mouth lifted to his, Jake knew he truly had
come home.

To the boy who wanted him to be his father. And to the
woman who had never stopped loving him.

If you enjoyed what you just read,
then we've got an offer you can't resist!

Take 2 bestselling love stories FREE!

Plus get a FREE surprise gift!

Clip this page and mail it to Harlequin Reader Service®

IN U.S.A.	**IN CANADA**
3010 Walden Ave.	P.O. Box 609
P.O. Box 1867	Fort Erie, Ontario
Buffalo, N.Y. 14240-1867	L2A 5X3

YES! Please send me 2 free Harlequin Presents® novels and my free surprise gift. After receiving them, if I don't wish to receive anymore, I can return the shipping statement marked cancel. If I don't cancel, I will receive 6 brand-new novels every month, before they're available in stores! In the U.S.A., bill me at the bargain price of $3.80 plus 25¢ shipping & handling per book and applicable sales tax, if any*. In Canada, bill me at the bargain price of $4.47 plus 25¢ shipping & handling per book and applicable taxes**. That's the complete price and a savings of at least 10% off the cover prices—what a great deal! I understand that accepting the 2 free books and gift places me under no obligation ever to buy any books. I can always return a shipment and cancel at any time. Even if I never buy another book from Harlequin, the 2 free books and gift are mine to keep forever.

106 HDN DZ7Y
306 HDN DZ7Z

Name	(PLEASE PRINT)	
Address	Apt.#	
City	State/Prov.	Zip/Postal Code

Not valid to current Harlequin Presents® subscribers.

Want to try two free books from another series?
Call 1-800-873-8635 or visit www.morefreebooks.com.

* Terms and prices subject to change without notice. Sales tax applicable in N.Y.
** Canadian residents will be charged applicable provincial taxes and GST.
   All orders subject to approval. Offer limited to one per household.
   ® are registered trademarks owned and used by the trademark owner and or its licensee.

PRES04R   ©2004 Harlequin Enterprises Limited

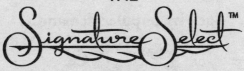
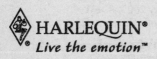

The world's bestselling romance series.

Seduction and Passion Guaranteed!

They're the men who have everything—except a bride....

Wealth, power, charm—what else could a heart-stoppingly handsome tycoon need? In the GREEK TYCOONS miniseries you have already been introduced to some gorgeous Greek multimillionaires who are in need of wives.

THE GREEK BOSS'S DEMAND
by *Trish Morey*
On sale January 2005, #2444

THE GREEK TYCOON'S CONVENIENT MISTRESS
by *Lynne Graham*
On sale February 2005, #2445

THE GREEK'S SEVEN-DAY SEDUCTION
by *Susan Stephens*
On sale March 2005, #2455

Pick up a Harlequin Presents® novel and you will enter a world of spine-tingling passion and provocative, tantalizing romance!

Available wherever Harlequin books are sold.

www.eHarlequin.com

HPTGTY0105